THOSE CRAZY CAMERA GUYS

THOSE CRAZY CAMERA GUYS

Navy combat photographers in Vietnam

Ken Bumpus

Order this book online at www.trafford.com
or email orders@trafford.com

Most Trafford titles are also available at major online book retailers.

All characters depicted in this narrative are fictional and imaginary. Any resemblance to persons, living or dead, is purely coincidental and unintended.

The incidents related here are based on a few experiences of the author and various other "sea stories", "rumors" and "tall tales" passed on to him by friends and shipmates. ALL said incidents are of questionable truth and have been played with, doctored, and altered to fit the tone of this fictional novel.

The Author

Printed in the United States of America.

ISBN: 978-1-4669-0623-5 (sc)
ISBN: 978-1-4669-0622-8 (e)

Trafford rev. 12/08/2011

 www.trafford.com

North America & international
toll-free: 1 888 232 4444 (USA & Canada)
phone: 250 383 6864 ♦ fax: 812 355 4082

Dedicated with deep appreciation to my wife, EVA, for her encouragement and patience during my struggles with writing this novel, and, especially for her assistance in correcting my many grammatical, spelling and punctuation errors.

K.

ONE

An intense feeling of relief swept over Senior Chief Photographer's Mate 'Buster' Brady as he thought back over these last few months. It wasn't fear of getting killed, wounded or captured that had haunted him throughout this tour—God, No!—This was the third war he'd been through in his 25 years as a Navy photographer. It was this screwball bunch with whom he'd spent these months as father-confessor, nursemaid and watchdog that had kept him popping Rolaids

It took only a few weeks in Vietnam to convince him that he most likely would not be getting out unscathed. Yet, here he was, his rotation date had arrived, and he had his butt comfortably planted in a well-upholstered seat of a military chartered PanAm 737 climbing rapidly away from Tan Son Nhut airport.

The fact he was going home instead of to the Navy Brig in Portsmouth, or that he was still a Senior Chief and not busted back to Airman Recruit, was some kind of miracle.

'Those Crazy Camera Guys', as they'd come to be known throughout Southeast Asia, kept the veteran Chief in a constant sweat with their high-jinks and their brink-of-illegal shenanigans—not that they were crooked or bad. They just had their own way of getting things done which skirted the red tape of 'the Navy way' with wild abandon and side-stepped 'Navy Regs' right and left.

All the men in his Combat Camera Group team were specialists in their field when it came to getting the images of war on film, at the same time struggling under the pressures of the bureaucratic limitations placed on fighting this 'war'. With their 'to hell with rules' attitude, they were experts at getting the job done while ignoring restrictions.

"Would you like a Coke?"

He was startled out of his reflections and looked up to see an attractive brunette in a PanAm uniform offering him a <u>real</u> 'stateside' Coke. He recognized it as a 'real stateside' Coke because the ice was crystal clear, not brown, and there were no little creatures frozen within.

"Thanks, I sure would," he said and guzzled it thirstily.

As he enjoyed the coolness replacing the heat and sweat he'd just left on the ground in the steaming humidity of Saigon, he looked around at the other members of his team.

The men of Team Alpha-One were scattered throughout the cabin of the plane, trying their best to look calm and unexcited. Chief Brady knew better, though, because, living as close as they had during the many months just passed, he had come to know the moods lying just beneath the surface. That apparent calmness each of them displayed was a cover for their true emotions. It was a trick they had learned out of necessity, to keep from losing their sanity while in 'Nam. It was the shield thrown up between them and the horrors and frustrations they encountered daily in this crazy "war".

Some of the guys learned quickly what others took weeks to come to understand just how 'the system' worked in Vietnam. About having to 'hunker down' while taking enemy fire and waiting for some 'big-shot' brass, sitting in some far off command post, to give them permission to return fire.

It was probably 'Mad Man' Jerry Madison who showed the rest of the men the answer to keeping their 'cool'—by outwardly appearing unconcerned and looking for, and finding, little bits of humor in even the most grotesque situation. This was his secret which eventually infected the others, giving them the ability to continue to function under extreme stress.

'Mad Man' had acquired his name, not because of the obvious last name tie-in, but because he just couldn't take anything serious. Not even war!

He's a natural clown and claims to know every Henny Youngman one-liner and probably 20,000 to 30,000 Bob Hope punch lines. He was raised near Las Vegas and spent a good share of his growing-up years sneaking backstage at the casinos to watch and study all the big time comedians perform. It was there he honed his comedic attitude.

Mad Man's ability to find something funny in any situation put him out of reach of the awful events taking place all around him.

This was the attitude that all the Combat Camera team and many others finally adopted to get them through the ordeal. A kind of 'Sad Sack/Gomer Pyle' approach, which must have worked, because, here they were, on their way home, safe and (moderately) sane!

In the seat one row back was Photographer's Mate First Class 'A.J.' Jameson, the biggest among them at 6'3" and 225 pounds. A teddy-bear of a man, tough but gentle. He had one weakness however—he was highly sensitive about his real first name. He had been tagged with an old family name—'Aloysious', and guarded the secret with threats of extreme bodily harm to anyone foolish enough to speak it.

Further back sat Rico 'Little Caesar' Cessario. He was the 'scrounger' of the team. Anytime there was some piece of equipment, an essential part, weapons, jungle fatigues, or non-regulation transport, which wasn't obtainable through regular channels,—'Little Caesar' was the man to "locate and liberate" it. Rico enjoyed this role because, being from a farm just south of Chicago, he fancied himself as having close ties to the Chicago mobs (not true.)

The quiet one across the aisle was David 'Ding-a-Ling' Lin, a Chinese-American from Hollywood. The son of a Hollywood cinematographer who had apprenticed under James Wong Howe, David had chosen to gain his photographic training by obtaining a BA degree in Cinematography from U.S.C. There he became friends with some of the Navy photographers going through a special Navy motion picture director training program. Upon graduation, in order to avoid being drafted, he decided to join the Naval Reserve and went on active duty to fulfill his military obligations.

It was in 'boot camp' that he received his nickname, when another recruit found out he left Hollywood for the Navy.

His comment was: "You know, I always said California was the 'Granola' state—what isn't fruits or nuts is flakey. You left 'Hollywierd' with all that delicious pussy for this fucked up outfit? What a ding-a-ling." The name stuck!

The fifth and final member of Team Alpha One was in the rear of the cabin keeping three of the flight attendants enthralled with his 'down-home' stories of life in the backwoods of northeast "Gawgia".

Photographer's Mate Second Class Donald "Redneck" Reddick was 'born and reared' in the red-clay hills of Georgia where he acquired the slowest, broadest southern drawl ever heard in the US Navy. He had managed to learn every four-letter word in existence and had invented numerous combinations and variations un-thought of by any other living soul.

It was said, that, in 'boot-camp' he hooked up with another 'rebel' from South Alabama who had to translate for him until he was able to speak enough english to communicate with the other recruits

These were the men Senior Chief Brady had come to love and admire.

The **Pacific Fleet Combat Camera Group** had been formed back in San Diego during the 'Police Action' in Korea and, Senior Chief Brady's was one of the teams put on 'stand-by' when the military presence in South Vietnam still consisted of only 'advisors'. Very shortly, they were on a flight to the Far East Combat Camera Group Detachment Alpha based in Japan.

Shortly after arriving in Yokosuka, things started heating up in the cities and jungles of 'Nam.

On March 8th the 9th Marine Expeditionary Brigade put the initial combat troops ashore at a point near Da Nang dubbed 'Red Beach'. Senior Chief Brady and his five-man team were put on 'red alert'. It was for sure, if things continued to boil, there would be a need for their talents.

The buildup progressed rapidly after the landing. and the Navy established a 7th Fleet Admin Detachment in Saigon and support staff personnel began to pour into the country. It wasn't long before the team was given their orders—

The team was going to war!

Well,—almost!

First they would have to get there, get established and check-in with the Senior Navy command (ComNavForV) in Saigon—IF they could find their offices in this strange land with an even stranger language—a conglomeration of Vietnamese/ Chinese/French/ and 'Pidgin English'.

They caught their Flight out of Tachikawa, southeast of Tokyo, in the late afternoon and, on their arrival after dark at Tan Son Nhut Aeroport, they found the Navy Personnel Check-In desk unmanned.

"Where the hell is everybody?" Mad Man inquired of no one in particular.

"They go dee dee mau to Saigon. Soon curfew," a young Vietnamese boy replied.

"This is the shits, Senior Chief. What are we supposed to do, now?" Rico 'Little Caesar' Cessario asked.

"Well, I guess we do what we always do in a case like this," Senior Chief Brady answered.

"And what in the hell is that, pray tell? Ask Travelers' Aid?" chimed in Mad Man.

"We fall back and punt, you dumb asshole," Photographer's Mate First Class 'A.J.' Jameson added. "If you think we're going to lie around in this terminal all night your brain's already pickled from the heat."

"You're right A.J. We gotta get off our butts and find a safe place to hunker down for the night. I sure don't think this place fits that bill." said Brady. "It's too damn open and exposed with little or no protection. Even the rats in this barn crawl into their holes and keep their heads down."

"You're fuck'n 'A' right about that, Chief," said Little Caesar, "I heard on the AFRS news a couple days ago, that, just last week, the VC planted a satchel charge near the Air France office across the way and blew the hell out of this place.

"They still haven't repaired all the damage. You can still see some of the frag holes and blood splatters on the wall you're leaning against there, Ding-a-ling."

Ding-a-Ling Lin sprang away from the wall like it was still red-hot from the blast.

'Ding-a-Ling' didn't much like his nickname, but from his CCG teammates, he came to accept it as a friendly term, and had learned to live with it.

"Well, let me see if I can jack up somebody and get us out of here and settled in for the night." Chief Brady said. "We gotta do something or we'll be stuck here when curfew goes down, then we'll really be shit out of luck, for sure, for sure."

"Hey, Chief, how about that UPI photographer you said you know? Isn't he supposed to be 'in country' somewhere?" Mad Man asked.

"Hey, yeah, Madison, I'm glad you reminded me of that. I'll see if I can find a phone around here that understands English. I know I have his Saigon number somewhere in my handy-dandy little black book of useful information. You guys sit tight here and park on our gear, while I do some reconnoitering—that means 'checky-checky', Rico."

And the Chief was off.

After a few minutes he managed to locate a telephone behind one of the deserted passenger check-in counters. It looked to be almost as ancient as the old man picking through a nearby trash barrel, but, after dialing the number, it appeared to be in working order. The phone on the other end rang several times before it was picked up and a sleeping voice answered.

"Yeah?"

"This is Senior Chief Brady with the Navy photo team. Is Nelson there?"

"Hey, what d'ya say, 'Buster'? No, Nelson is out in the 'boonies' for a couple of days. This is O'Brian. We met in 'Frisco a couple years ago. You were tipping back a few 'cool-ones' with Nelson that night. You were on some sort of a photo shoot at the Oakland Navy Supply Depot, as I recall."

"Hell yes, I remember you, O'Brian. You helped me haul ol' Nels back to his hotel later that night and pour him into the sack."

"What the heck are you doing in this hole at this time of night, Chief?"

"Well, I've got my five-man team of misfit photo mates with me, and the Navy contact desk out here at Tan Son Nhut has boogied out for the night. His counter is closed up tighter than a drum. They've all gone home leaving us with a problem of finding a place to park our bones for the night. Got any decent hotels in this burg you can recommend?"

"I'll do you one better, Chief. With Nelson and the other two shutterbugs out of town, we have three empty bunks right here. I'm all alone in this big room. You can squeeze up and there'll be plenty of room for you and your guys."

"Hey, GREAT! How do we find you?"

"Just grab one of those yellow and blue Renault cabs and tell the driver: 'Mai Khan Hotel.' They all know where it is. Make sure he doesn't try to charge more than 15 piastres per man, though. There are a few of those wheel-jockeys who'll try to get rich off any 'first-timer' 'round eyes', so make like you know your way around and he'll be happy for the late-night fare. Not many people are out this time of the night—except the VC, and they don't usually travel by cab. (but don't count on that, either.)"

"Geez, thanks Podner. You're a life saver. We'll see you in a little while."

"Don't mention it, Buster. I'll be glad for some company. Have a safe trip."

After getting the guys and all the gear together, Chief Brady sent A. J. and Mad Man off to round up a taxi.

"You men are going to have to 'hot-bunk' it in my friend's hotel room, but you might as well get used to 'making do'. Even in this big city they call 'The Paris of The Orient.', we won't find many of the comforts of home—not by a long shot!"

"Chief, the way I feel right now, I'll be happy to sleep hanging from the chandelier—if the room has one," said Ding-a-Ling.

"Yeah. anything is better than we'll find when we get out in the 'boonies,'" Little Caesar added.

"Tomorrow we'll scout for more permanent digs. The first thing we'll have to do in the morning is check in at the Navy command here and let them know we're on the job. We need to get the 'skinny' on how things are run down here." Brady said.

About that time Mad Man showed up shaking his head.

"Chief, you won't believe what they call 'taxis' in this town. They're not much bigger than roller skates. At first we thought maybe we should hire one for each foot but we settled on three that looked like they'll hold together long enough to get us to town. A. J. is holding them for us out front. They're anxious to get moving, so we'd best load up and, as the kid says,: 'dee dee mau'. I found out that means 'haul our asses out of here.'"

Quickly gathering their stuff, they trooped off to where the taxis waited. It took a bit of squeezing and shoving, but, with A. J. finally snuggled up to the camera cases in one cab, Little Caesar with the luggage in the second, and Chief Brady and the other three men in the third, the parade set off for Saigon.

A. J.'s taxi led the pack with the driver who seemed to understand English best—which wasn't saying much. However, when given the name of the hotel, he grinned broadly and shook his head; "Sure, Joe, Mai Khan, me know. We hurry. Beat curfew!"

With that said, the taxi shot from the curb like a scalded pup, barely avoiding swapping fenders with an ARVN army jeep that seemed to also be rocket propelled.

"Hey, man. Wait for the others. Don't lose them. And I <u>would</u> like to get there in one piece, please!"

"They come, too. All drivers know Mai Khan. We get there OK. Me 'Numba one' driver. You betcha."

With screaming tires, blaring horns, the caravan dodged in and out among the rickshaws, cyclos (3-wheeled motorcycles), Vespa motor scooters (carrying whole families), other taxis and various military vehicles. To the newcomers, it seemed their drivers were missing collisions with fractions of an inch to spare.

"You know, fella," Little Caesar shouted above the traffic racket at his driver. "If this jalopy had one more coat of paint we'd be bouncing off everything on the street!"

"I swear, these drivers must have learned to drive in the Compton Demolition Derby!" Chief Brady commented. "We could wind up in body bags right here and never make it into Saigon!"

"Chief, I've been on the L.A. Freeways, New York's Eastside Highway, and the Piazza Municipio in Naples, but their traffic doesn't hold a candle to this for ass-puckering thrills!"

"Know what you mean, Mad Man, and I couldn't agree more. I'm relearning how to pray, again. This is like nothing I've ever experienced in my lifetime."

Ding-a-Ling had a grip so tight on the dash panel that his fingerprints would forever be embossed into the plastic.

"I almost wish we'd walked instead of taking this roller-coaster through hell," he said. "Although that doesn't look like it would be much safer. All the pedestrians are zigging and zagging through the traffic like Joe Namouth working his way through the Green Bay backfield. This is the real 'suicide alley', if you ask me."

After what seemed like an eternity, the taxis, with squealing tires and smoking brake pads, pulled up in front of a middle class (for Saigon) hotel. Surprisingly they arrived within minutes of each other, attesting to either the expertise <u>or</u> the astounding good luck of their drivers. The team members rolled out of the cabs, thoroughly shaken up, mentally as well as physically. All of them breathed a sigh of relief and, after a few minutes to get steady on their feet, quickly began unloading their gear and muscling it into the hotel lobby, hand-to-hand chain-style.

Chief Brady found his friend, O'Brian, waiting for them.

"Glad to see you made it before curfew, Buster," he greeted him.

"Damn, O'Brian, we're glad we made it at <u>all</u>! You could have warned us about these Kamikaze drivers. It's going to take a week's soaking and five washings to get our skivvies clean, again!"

"Ha, that's something every man has to experience for himself. There is no way I could have described it to you, that you would have believed! Call it your initiation to 'Nam, Pal."

"That was exhausting. Hope you have a cold beer in your room. We could all do with a little 'nerve medicine' about now."

"Man, you ever hear of old Nelson without a good stash of refreshments? Come on up to the room. He'll be glad to share it with you. That's one item that's plentiful and cheap out here.

"It's always good to run into old friends in this bit of Hell!" O'Brian added. "There's one thing everyone learns in 'Nam and that's the value of friends. Too many of them aren't around very long."

The door slammed open and Petty Officer Madison and Little Caesar stumbled into the room loaded down with camera gear and luggage.

"Senior Chief, it's a damn good thing this hotel has an elevator. Me and Little Caesar would be ready for a week with the chiropractor if we'd had to horse this stuff up those five floors on our backs. A. J., Redneck, and Ding-a-Ling will be here with the rest of our junk in a minute."

"OK, Mad Man, just stack the camera gear in the corner. You guys can worry about sorting out your personal luggage later."

"Hey, O'Brian, coming up in the elevator just now, we could hear 'booming' sounds. What was that?" Little Caesar asked.

"Well, that depends. If it was sporadic and intermittent, it was 'Charlie' with his nightly mortar soirée into the suburbs. But—if it was rhythmic with a heavy back beat, it was probably the juke-box in the night club up on the roof."

"Holy shit! You mean to say you got your own juke-joint right here on the roof of the Mai Khan?" A. J. whooped.

"Yeah, such as it may be. But it get's to jumpin' after curfew when everybody has to get off the street and hole up inside."

Mad Man jumped up from the cot where he had collapsed and said: "I'm rested! Let's hit the joint for some cool ones right now! Anybody with me?"

Little Caesar, A. J., Ding-a-Ling, and Redneck all made a wild dash for the door, almost knocking each other over in the charge.

"Hey, guys," Chief Brady shouted after them, "You best not stay out too late. We've got a lot to do tomorrow and I don't want a bunch of casualties nursing hangovers that'll put you out of shape for doing a 'squared-away' day's work.

"I guess it's pretty safe up there, isn't it?" he turned to O'Brian.

"Oh, sure. As safe as anywhere in this crazy town. If I want a drink and enjoy some stateside music that's the only place I'll go. I don't 'bar-hop' much. Too many 'incidents' out there. Drop your guard for an instant and you get a fast trip back to the ConUS, with a flag draped over you.

"I don't cotton to those Tu Do Street bar girls, and I don't 'do the town' when the other guys are away. I'm the office flunky so I'm stuck here jockeying a desk, getting their stuff 'on the wire' when they come back with their stories and film."

"Sounds like you miss out on all the adventure, Pal."

"Don't you believe it Buster! There's more 'adventure' right here on the streets of Saigon than I'll need in my lifetime! There's shootings and bombings some place close-by 24-hours a day. Sometimes I believe I'm in more danger here than the photogs and journalists who go out on patrols in the rice-paddies and jungles with the 'grunts'. It's anything <u>but</u> boring!

"Chief, I'd advise you to brief your crew about getting around. safely, in this town,.

Just a few pointers: This war is not like any other. We call it a 'commuter's war', 'cause almost everybody lives in billets (hotels taken over by the military) in town or in the base camps close by. In the morning they harness up and go out on their 'search and destroy' missions and are back in a few hours (if they make it) or couple of days, and are eating hot grub and sleeping in clean beds.

"I don't mean to imply that there aren't a whole lot of Marines and 'Grunts' sloshing around out there in the swamps and rice-paddies, and living in wet mud holes, eating 'C' rations. We see the body bags being loaded on the planes at Tan Son Nhut every day.

"But, what I want you to understand, Chief, is—some of those bags were filled right here in town by Victor Charley and his friends. They've been known to toss grenades and machine-gun our guys from vehicles as they stand, innocently trying to hail a cab. This is where 'drive-by' killings originated.

"So tell your guys not to stand around in groups and to space themselves out when they're walking on the sidewalks. We have one gal here who rides side-saddle behind her 'cowboy' (juvey VC) on a Vespa scooter and loves to 'frag' us 'round-eyes'. We call her 'Tiger Lil' and she hasn't been caught yet.

"Even shoe-shine boys have been caught with pistols and grenades among their cans of Shinola and Kiwi polish."

"Geez, O'Brian, I guess you're right. I'd best get my guys together first thing in the morning and give them the word. They're a pretty 'happy-go-lucky' bunch, which could mean trouble if they're not clued in. I want them all to go back with all their parts still together when this tour is over. Thanks! for the heads-up, Pal."

TWO

THE CREW, WITH some exceptions, slept fitfully because of the unfamiliar sounds of war which were all too close for comfort.

Only Mad Man, Little Caesar, Ding-a-Ling, Redneck and A. J. had no trouble sleeping though. Probably due to the large amounts of beer consumed the night before.

The partying affected Ding-a-Ling more than the rest, due, no doubt, to the ratio of quantity consumed to body size.

"Man, that Vietnam beer sho' must be the VCs' secret weapon," Redneck drawled. "Ain't no wonder they call it 'Bomb-y-bomb'." Which drew laughs from Brady and O'Brian.

O'Brian set them straight, though. "'Bah Mi Bah', in Vietnamese, means '33'. Like it says on the bottle—'33'. But I know where of thou speaketh. Little Buddy. It has 'laid out many a poor man'. Just as effectively as an M-79 grenade. It's sure not your average stateside brewsky."

"OK, Sailors, listen up!" Chief Brady passed on O'Brian's warning about safety on the streets. Then said: "Our first mission for the day—as our orders say, we have to check in with the Headquarters Naval Support Activity personnel office to get our orders endorsed and get assigned a place to sleep tonight. Then we have to go over to COMUSMACV—that's Westmoreland's compound, it stands for <u>COM</u>mander <u>US</u> <u>M</u>ilitary <u>A</u>ssistance <u>C</u>ommand <u>V</u>ietnam. The Public Affairs Officer there will issue us our PRESS credentials. With those we can hitch rides on planes, trains or Jeeps all over 'Nam and we'll have unrestricted movement anywhere 'in country.'"

"Hey, Senior Chief," Little Caesar said. "Don't we get to have some chow? Last night left me with an appetite. I could eat a whole water buffalo, tail and all."

"Yeah, you're right. We'll take care of that, first off. Where do you suggest, O'Brian?"

"Well, you'll just be a couple of doors from NavSup if you go to 'Cheap Charlie's'. They serve a good breakfast, and, as the name suggests, the price is right. A lot of the Navy guys eat there rather than the official mess halls. Nobody has gotten ptomaine there, yet, so it must be OK. I know the food's good 'cause I eat there quite a lot, myself."

"OK. We'll give it a try. You want to come along?"

"Nah, I have to meet my guys at the office, shortly. They're due in this morning. Your stuff will be safe here and you can pick it up when you get your own digs. I'll leave word at the desk and you can just pick up a key whenever you want. Have a good day, now, and be careful. Watch your 'six.'"

"So long, Pal. We sure appreciate your hospitality. You've been a lifesaver. Maybe we can meet up later on and you and Nelson can hoist a few with us. Tell him 'hello' for me and I'll catch you both on the flip flop."

It was just four or five blocks from the Mai Khan to 'Cheap Charlie's' so the team decided to walk and not risk another ride in the 'Saigon Demolition Derby'—as Mad Man now called it.

As they walked by the Caravelle Hotel, where NBC, CBS, ABC and a lot of other reporters and correspondents, who worked for the 'big money outfits' (O'Brian's name for them), stayed, the Army MP on guard in the sand-bag bunker snapped a sharp salute to Senior Chief Brady, who returned it with a twinkle in his eye.

"Hey, Senior Chief," Little Caesar said. "He must notta' recognized your collar-devices and thought you were some kinda officer, huh?"

"Yeah, I thought it best to just go along with it, rather than embarrass him. He probably doesn't see too many fouled anchor insignia and wasn't going to take the risk of not saluting, just in case."

"Most of these 'Grunts' aren't too bright, anyway, or they'd be in the Navy, huh, Senior Chief?"

"Don't sell them short, Caesar. They do their job with just as much patriotism and skill as the rest of us."

The gang trouped into 'Cheap Charlie's', pushed tables together to accommodate everyone, and flopped down.

"Guys, I don't know much about Vietnamese cuisine," Brady said, "but if we have any problem ordering, we'll just point to what looks good on the other tables. That's always worked for me in the other countries where I've landed. Believe me, I've been in a lot of strange countries and had some strange food, but only once did I ever have to leave any grub on my plate."

"When was that, Senior Chief?" Ding-a-Ling asked.

"Well, I was in a hole-in-the-wall restaurant in Pusan, Korea in '51 and the waiter recommended quail in a wine gravy. It was a new one on me, but I said, 'OK,' I'd give it a try. At the time I was hungry enough to eat the south end of a north-bound skunk.

"It was really very tasty until I bit down on a piece of bone—you sure you want to hear this before we eat, fellows?"

"Shit, Senior Chief, we all went through 'survival training school' and we ate some pretty odd food there. Go ahead."

"OK, Mad Man, you asked for it. Well, when I took the piece of 'bone' out of my mouth, I was looking at the 'quail's' beak and one beady little eye looking back at me."

"Gah! That's gross," Ding-a-Ling choked. "What didja' do?"

"I just took my fork and shoveled the remaining pieces around until I found the other half of the bird's head, set it aside and proceeded to enjoy the rest of my meal.

"With that said, I guess we ought to order—if anyone's still hungry."

"You ain't gonna' keep me away from the grub with a story like that," said A.J..

As a group they all opted for the 'breakfast special' recommended by an Army SFC (Sergeant First Class) sitting at a nearby table.

When the waiter brought the meal to their table, it turned out to be a sort of custard dish, served at the table 'a flambé'.

Seeing the waiter set his breakfast on fire, Mad Man grabbed his coffee cup and was about to douse the flames, when A.J. stopped him and explained that was just the rum or brandy on top that was afire, and it'd burn off in a minute and leave a tasty crust on the custard.

When Mad Man calmed down, the gang 'turned to' and made short work of their breakfast, and were pleasantly surprised to discover that it was just as advertised—good—and 'Cheap'.

With their appetites appeased, the team proceeded to the Naval Support Activity Office to check in and be assigned berthing—that proved to be very quick and simple—<u>there was no</u> <u>berthing</u> <u>or</u> <u>messing</u> available!

"You guys are mobile and we can't tie up what rooms we have, when your orders say you'll be tramping all over 'Nam. We don't know when you'll need the rooms and when they'll be standing vacant." the LTjg Billeting Officer told Brady.

"Understood, Lieutenant. But what are we supposed to do for a bunk while we <u>are</u> in Saigon, Sir?"

"The best I can do is endorse your orders 'No Berthing or Messing Available' and you'll go on per diem, Senior Chief."

"How does that solve the problem, Lt.?"

"Well, you'll have to use the per diem money and rent hotel rooms and purchase your meals in an open mess or at local restaurants, I guess. 'Sorry 'bout that,'" he said with a smile.

"Yeah, I've watched 'Get Smart', too, Lieutenant, but I really can't appreciate the humor, right now."

It took a while to surmount the 'red tape' and get all their orders stamped and signed. But when it was all cleared up, Senior Chief Brady and CCG Detachment Alpha-One loaded aboard pedicabs (1/2 motorcycle, 1/2 rickshaw) and headed for the COMUSMACV compound.

"I sure hope they don't screw with us here, too, Chief," was Mad Man's wry comment. "We'll never get anything done, at this rate."

Their luck changed at this stop, however. The Public Affairs Officer for COMUSMACV just happened to be an old shipmate of Brady's from Korea, Lieutenant Commander O. P. Duff.

With this going for them it shortened the work of getting their Press accreditation cleared. They all had their photos taken and the cards finished up in less than an hour which gave them a good part of the afternoon to book rooms for tonight.

By getting to the Mai Khan shortly after lunch, they were able to get two adjoining rooms, with the bath just two doors down the hall.

"You very lucky," the Vietnamese desk clerk said. "By 1600 (4 PM) we get many men look for rooms. Very busy then. No rooms left. All full up."

The men spent the rest of the afternoon moving their camera equipment and luggage from Nelson's room to theirs on the sixth floor.

"Hey, this is great!" said Mad Man, "Now we won't have so far to go to get to the roof-top party room. How 'bout that?"

"Don't make too many plans, Madison," The Chief told him, "I've got to check with the 7th Fleet Detachment office for our assignment. We may be pulling out in the morning. Don't forget we're here to work, Guys."

THREE

Just as Senior Chief Brady had guessed, the team was directed to hop a flight first thing in the morning to Da Nang and hook up with the CBs (Construction Battalion) there. They were beginning construction on a hospital across the Han River from Da Nang, where the casualties from I Corps (the northern sector command of South Vietnam), would be treated.

On arrival, the team made it's first stop at the 'White Elephant', a former French Army hospital, being temporarily used by the Navy for administrative services offices. Senior Chief Brady informed the Personnel Officer of the team's assignment and then set about locating transport to the CB camp across the river.

He finally located a CB truck that was about ready to leave and talked the driver, BU2 (Builder Second Class) Shaunessy, into giving them a lift. Everyone pitched-in and had the gear loaded in double-quick time. By then, it was almost dusk and the driver advised them they'd best 'dee dee mau' before it got dark.

"We sure don't want to be on the road or crossing that river after dark," Shaunessy said. "That's the VCs' favorite time to pull an ambush. They come out of nowhere and hit-and-run."

The trip, though rough, went well until they arrived at the rickety bridge crossing the river.

"This is where everybody gets out and walks," said the grizzled CB. "This bridge might not handle all of you, plus your gear. It's been known to drop a wheel through the planks if we strain it too much."

"OK," said Brady, "All ashore what's goin' ashore. And, if you have to go into the water, keep those weapons high and dry and swim for the south shore! Keep your eyes and ears peeled for any movement on either bank. We're sitting ducks out here, so don't drag ass or you might get it blown off!"

"Thanks for those encouraging words, Senior Chief," Little Caesar shouted above the roar of the truck's engine. "We'll remember them as we're med-evaced back to 'The World'."

Everyone made it across safely and then it was up to Petty Officer Shaunessy to maneuver the big truck over the flimsy bridge. He was almost across when the sound of splintering wood warned of trouble. He nonchalantly threw the truck into 4-wheel drive and gunned the motor. It made a jack-rabbit leap forward and cleared the bridge just as it gave way.

"Well, I guess we'll have to get a crew out here in the morning to re-plank that sombitch." he said. "One good thing, though, if 'Charlie' wants to come across to harass us tonight, he'll have to swim. There's no other bridge for ten miles up or down stream."

"Tell me, Shaunessy, this CB Detachment has been here for two months, now. How come, with all you 'hammer-swingers' you haven't put together a decent bridge?"

"Senior Chief, we figure, if we make it too good, 'Charlie' will be able to move his heavy stuff to this side of the river and make _real_ trouble for us—which we sure don't need while we're trying to build this hospital. Then, again, he just might blow it up for the fun of it, and we're no better off. It'll just be a waste of valuable materials and work-time. Why give 'Charlie' that pleasure. We'd rather keep it the way it is so they'll have as much trouble crossing as we do. This way they can't come across with too big a force or they'll all wind-up in the drink. Even 'Charlie' doesn't relish a swim in that polluted cesspool!"

"Leave it to a CB to come up with reasoning like that," Mad Man commented.

"Hey, when you've been 'in country' for a while, you learn to conserve every ounce of energy and depend on the ol' melon." Shaunessy came back.

The rest of the trip to the CB camp went off without a hitch and the photo team was treated to a hot cooked meal, a bath with fresh water from a 'water buffalo (a tank-trailer), and assigned to cots in 'hard-back' barracks tents (a canvas tent over a 2x4 framework). Senior Chief Brady and A.J. were put up in a tent with the CB chiefs, and, as pooped as they were from the flight and the truck ride, it was only minutes until they were all snoring in chorus with the CBs.

Their peaceful sleep didn't last long, though. Brady and A.J. were brought wide awake with the sound of nearby explosions, followed by the hissing of sand raining down on the canvas roof! Both men sat bolt upright on their cots and prepared to make a run for the bunker just outside the door.

Their flight was halted when, by the light filtering into the tent from the perimeter floodlights, they noted all the CB chiefs hadn't stirred and were still 'sawing logs'.

The two men just looked at each other, shrugged, and laid back down and tried to ignore the 'whump! whump!' outside the tent, and attempt to get back to sleep.

In the morning, at breakfast, they found out why no alarm had been sounded.

Brady asked the CB Command Master Chief, and drew a smile from him.

"Hell," he said, "That's those damn 'Jarheads' across the road in that Marine Helo Air Wing Landing pad. Their sentries keep thinkin' they see VC sneaking down the road in the dark, so they open fire with their M-79 grenade launchers (sort of pregnant shotguns). The only trouble, they're 'flyboy' Marines, and they hardly know which end of the thing to point at the target. In the two months this camp has been here, they still haven't zeroed-in on the road and they keep dropping them into our inner perimeter. Luckily that's about the limit of the range for an M-79. So far they haven't hit anything—VC <u>or</u> CB! So we just ignore 'em. Our CO raises hell about it every so often but, you see how much good that does."

The rest of the day the team spent scouting the hospital construction site and shooting some preliminary footage. Part of the construction project involved operating a rock crusher the CBs had assembled up on the side of 'Monkey Mountain'.

They would be needing the gravel produced for concrete they'd be pouring later.

Chief Brady thought some shots of that operation could be an essential part of the story, so, the next morning he bummed a vehicle and loaded up the crew and camera equipment and, with some directions from one of the CB Chiefs, they took off for the mountain.

The road up the mountain wound back and forth through the jungle, and suddenly, the photographers found out why it was called 'Monkey Mountain'! Out of the jungle came spine-tingling screams and hollering, like they'd never heard before. Startled, Chief Brady slowed the vehicle, thinking someone was in deep trouble.

As it happened, <u>they</u> were the 'someone' in trouble. The truck had slowed almost to a halt, when, out of the jungle charged a dozen or so monkeys, making the most awful ruckus ever heard! Brady immediately downed-shifted and tromped on the gas. As they sped away, they were pelted with rocks and sticks until they got out of range around a curve.

"It seems we've intruded on their domain, Senior Chief," remarked Ding-a-Ling.

"Them there lil' critters were downright cantankerous," Redneck said. "reminded of a possum I once treed and tried to grab him by the tail. Damn near took my thumb off."

"I'll sure remember, on the way back, not to slow down, I guarantee you!! Anyone hurt?"

"Nah, Chief," replied A.J., "Their aim ain't any better than those 'airdale' Marines back at camp."

Soon the jungle foliage began to thin out, and, the road emerged from the tree-line, revealing a large clearing where the rock crusher stood off to the side. Trucks and other heavy equipment were moving about and workers were busily feeding the large stones into the mouth of the crusher with a 'clamshell' crane.

Brady pulled their truck off the road and went to seek out the honcho-in-charge. A CB senior Chief, whom Brady and A.J. had shared a tent with the night before, walked over to him with his hand extended.

"Glad to see you shutterbugs survived the 'gauntlet'. I should have had someone warn you guys about that tribe of monkeys. If you aren't careful, they'll jump in your truck with you and they're damn vicious! One of our guys got his arm pretty badly chewed up back when we were turning that trail into a passable road. Had to fly him back to Saigon 'cause our hospital corpsman wasn't equipped to treat him here.

"Yeah, we learned real fast not to drag-ass through there," said Senior Chief Brady. "We thought for a minute, there, that we were being ambushed by 'Charlie.'"

"My name's Albee, Jim Albee." the CB said. "You're just in time for the big 'fireworks' show. Our 'powder monkey' is one of the best. He's set several charges in the quarry over there and he's about to blow them."

A shout of "FIRE IN THE HOLE!" followed by a siren warned them of the coming blast. Small pieces of rock fell all around the truck under which the CB and the photo team had sought refuge.

Ding-a-Ling picked up a baseball-size chunk of the rock and examined it.

"Hey, Chief! This is high grade <u>marble</u> they're using for gravel," he said.

"That's the same stuff all of these mountains, between here and Hoi An, are made of," Senior Chief Albee replied. "The Vietnamese have been digging it out for years to carve into tombstones, crucifixes, and statues. They discovered a new product to make after the troops started arriving. Just about every desk in the 'White Elephant' has a hand-carved marble nameplate displayed on it. The Vietnamese come in here every afternoon about quitting time and scrounge for pieces to haul home to carve and sell. We let them take whatever they can carry. Hell, there's plenty for all."

"Damn! I wish we'd gotten here 30 minutes earlier! That would have been a GREAT shot if we'd just had time to get set up," A.J. said.

"If you guys aren't in a big hurry, we'll be blowin' one more charge this afternoon," Chief Albee told Brady. "It'll take about an hour to drill the holes and another 45 minutes to an hour to stuff 'em."

"We'll stick around for it," Brady replied. "In the meantime, A.J., take Redneck and Ding-a-Ling and go shoot some film on the 'dozers, the 'clam-shell' and the crusher in operation. Plus anything else that looks good to you."

"Righto, Chief. 'Roger,' 'willco' and all that other affirmative, 'Yes, Sir' shit."

The wait turned out to be most productive. A.J., Redneck and Ding-a-Ling got about 500 feet of good stuff 'in the can'.

Chief Brady spent the time shooting black-and-white and Kodachrome stills and interviewing Albee and some of the other CBs, creating a photojournalistic piece to send back to ChInfo (Navy Chief of Information) in D.C., for release to the 'stateside' media.

"I think I got some good hometowners (news releases to a serviceman's hometown) as well as a story that could 'play' nationally," said Brady. "Now, let's find a safe place to set up our tripods. We need to anchor the cameras so we don't wind up with shaky images when that blast hits."

The second detonation was even more impressive than the first and gave the photographers just the pictures they needed. Late afternoon moved in and with it came the rain—the early introduction to the monsoons so common to this part of Southeast Asia. Driving back to the camp in the downpour was touch-and-go but Senior Chief Brady managed it without slipping off the mountainside.

"You know, Chief, I think that rain was a blessing in disguise," said Mad Man.

"At least, it kept the monkeys off our backs!"

FOUR

THREE MORE DAYS of work with the CBs pretty much wrapped up the initial phase of the hospital project so Chief Brady decided to call a recess.

"We need to spend some time on our other assignment in the Da Nang area. We'll let the CB project go until we can show some progress in it. Then we'll come back for more coverage. For now we need to go over to the 3rd MAF (Marine Assault Force). Their Public Affairs Officer wants us to provide some documentation of their ops."

The 3rd was located about a mile inland from Da Nang and their tents spread over 10 to 15 acres. Included in their small city was a helo pad and next to it a field aid station where the wounded were brought to be patched up. The more serious casualties, after being stabilized, were flown off shore to the Navy Hospital Ship Haven.

Brady's group were kept busy filming the medical teams bringing young Marines back to life and trying to put mangled bodies back together. Along with that, and photographing other marine activities in the camp, two days passed by quickly. The senior medical officer approached Brady and asked him:

"Would your team like to accompany a couple of my medics to a nearby village where they'll set up a temporary clinic to inoculate the locals and treat them for their minor aches and pains? I think it could help show the folks back home, some of the 'people to people' humanitarian work we're doing over here. It ain't all killing and maiming."

With a Navy doctor, an enlisted dental technician, a Third Class Hospital Corpsman, three Marine riflemen as escorts, and an ARVN (South Vietnamese) Sergeant as scout and interpreter, the caravan trooped off to the village.

The area was supposed to be VC-free but, just the same, walking down the jungle trails and along the dikes in the rice paddies, everyone was on high alert.

A.J. was startled by a small snake slithering across the dike in front of him and let out a yell. One of the Marines ran up, made a grab for it, and caught it just as it was disappearing under the water.

"You must be nuts, Marine!? How do you know that thing isn't poisonous? I see he managed to draw blood from your finger. I been told they have a lot of really deadly snakes over here. The green bamboo snake and one they call a 'One Step' are both real bad-asses. If they get ahold of you, they'll drop you in your tracks in the blink of an eyeball!"

"Hell, Man, I've handled all kinda snakes since I was a little squirt. I've been bitten several times and I ain't dead, yet!"

"I hope you're right this time, Jack, 'cause you're sure too damn big for even me to pack out of here. I've got enough to carry with this tripod, camera and extra film. I don't need no dumb, dead Marine to have to lug around!"

KAWOOMB! KAWOOMB!—The paddy exploded into a shower of mud and water.

"BUG OUT, BUG OUT!!" The Marine in the rear yelled. "Those are VC mortars and they're zeroing in on us. Head for cover!"

Twenty yards ahead of them was thick jungle and they all covered the distance in a mad rush following the lead Marine on a zig-zag path until they were deep into th brush before he held up his hand to signal a halt.

"*Wow!*" he whispered to Senior Chief Brady. "*Where did those little bastards come from? Our patrols ran a sweep through this neighborhood just last night, and it was supposed to be clean. I'm going to call this in and get a S & D (search and destroy) mission dropped in here. Those 'gooks' will probably fade before we can get some grunts in here, but we'll still have to find another route home when we finish.*"

"*Chief, I'm kinda' glad for all the mud 'cause it hides what I just deposited in my fatigues,*" Mad Man commented.

"*Don't feel lonely. My boots are full of what I hope and pray is rice-paddy mud,*" added Caesar.

"*Quitcher belly aching, you guys, and let's get on with our job and get back to the 3rd. I want to get a bath and get into some clean skivvies,*" was Ding-a-Ling's admonition.

"*WHOOEE!*" Redneck, whispered, "*That was a real pisser, eh, guys?*"

The word had gotten out that 'the doctor come today' so there was quite a welcoming party that greeted the jittery group.

The medics quickly set up shop on a table outside the village chief's hootch and began treating his people for everything from an impacted wisdom tooth to lancing a boil on one ancient 'papa-san's' wrinkled, leathery posterior. The medical team was kept busy as were the photographers and ultimately the Marine Corporal told the doctor:

"Sir, if we're going to make it back before dark, which we damn well better—excuse the slip of the tongue, Doc—we'd best saddle up and clear out. Our ARVN says he can take us back by another trail, but it's about a 'click' (kilometer) farther so it'll take longer going home than it did getting here."

"OK. Let's move it out, troops! You're the boss out here, Corporal."

The tents of the 3rd MAF were a welcome sight when the small force topped a hill and sighted the twinkling lights of the sprawling olive-drab community in the fading daylight.

The mess tent was open when they came into camp so the patrol dropped their gear off at their cots and headed that way to get some hot grub.

"Those C-rats we had to eat at noon may be nourishing but they sure leave a lot to be desired when it comes down to flavor."

"You got that right, A.J.!" said Mad Man. "They all taste like last month's left-overs. The only one that's even half-way palatable are those 'beanie weenies'. Those stale crackers came in handy the other day, though. That day we had to wait near the Da Nang airport and those helos kept landing and taking off and stirred up all that sand right outside the tent. I found that, if I ate crackers along with my canned corned beef, I couldn't tell if I was crunching sand or crackers!"

"Let's be glad we're getting hot, cooked chow, tonight, guys." Chief Brady said, "We should count our few blessings."

"Right, Chief."

After thoroughly enjoying their meal, the team returned to their tent and spent the evening cleaning their cameras and weapons, and reloading both. for whatever lay ahead tomorrow.

"Excuse me, guys," Mad Man said. "I gotta make head-run. My back teeth are floating."

"Hold up, I'll go with you."

"Caesar, it's not that I'd be embarrassed to share the trough with you, but I'd best warn you—don't stand too close. When I was a baby, our family doctor insisted on circumcising me, but the sumbitch was slightly cross-eyed and cut on a bias. Now every time I piss I have to stand sideways to the urinal to keep from filling up the pocket of anyone standing next to me."

"Mad man, you lie like a rug." Caesar replied.

"Oh, Yeah? Just get too close and you'll find out!"

"Senior Chief, have you ever heard such bull-shit?" Ding-a-Ling asked.

"Can't say as I have, but, it might be interesting to see if Madison's making up one of his usual ridiculous tall tales, or, if it might just be true this time. You want to check it out for us, Ding-a-Ling, be my guest."

"No thanks! My curiosity goes only so far, and I draw the line at inspecting how someone pees!"

"I think I'll wait 'til you get back," Caesar said. "I'm not that curious, either. I'll cross my legs for a while rather than take any chances."

With dawn came new challenges for the photographers. The Marine Public Affairs Officer offered the photo team a chance to accompany one of their day-light patrols into the jungle. "They'll take two of you along, but be sure your weapons are ready, 'cause you'll be expected to do some shooting, with them, as well as with your cameras, if you roust any VC."

"Chief, I'll go," offered A.J.

"Me too," Ding-a-Ling chimed in.

"OK, Guys, but I want stills as well as mopics so you each carry a Nikon and a pocket full of Tri-X and Kodachrome with you. And, for God's sake keep your butts down!

"Don't look so miserable, Mad Man, I'm sure the rest of us will get plenty of chances for 'guts and glory'—and probably all too soon! Just play it cool, like Redneck, there. It don't make a shit to him if he get's to play John Wayne, or not."

"You done got that right, Senior Chief. I figure the best way to keep from gettin' my ass shot off is not go stickin' it out!"

"OK, Get saddled up, fellas." the PAO ordered, "The sergeant said he'll meet you at 0900 at the mess tent. Good luck!"

The air in the photo team's tent crackled with excitement as A.J. and Ding-a-Ling gathered their packs and weapons. This would be Team Alpha-One's baptism of fire and everyone was praying for their success and safe return. Ding-a-Ling decided he'd carry a .45 as it would be easier to handle while filming with his Arriflex mopic camera. A.J., commenting that he preferred heavier fire-power, opted for a 'grease-gun' (a .45 caliber machine-gun resembling a mechanics grease gun). In A.J.'s big ham-like hands, even that looked mighty puny.

"Guys, remember—the pictures are important but <u>NOT</u> as important as you both coming back in one piece!" Brady warned them. "Good hunting, and God bless and protect you."

"See you later," Ding-a-Ling called back as they trooped off with the Marine 'Grunts'.

The mission, as it turned out, was to check out the same rice paddies where they'd drawn the mortar fire the day before and make a 360° sweep extending 250 meters out from the paddy edges.

"OK, you 'Swabbies'," the Marine squad leader said. "It's vital you keep your eyes sharp for any movement or anything that doesn't look right. These 'slope-heads' are tricky. They can hide in this jungle and you can walk within spittin' distance of them and never see 'em. Also, watch where you step. They love to plant trip-wires and 'punji' sticks and all sorts of 'boobie' traps along these trails. We've got a mighty sharp ARVN sergeant scouting for us and walking point, so we'd all be smart if we follow him and pay <u>close</u> attention to his signals. Got that?"

"Aye, Aye, Sarge." they both replied in unison.

Walking through the jungle while trying not to make noise was hard for the two camera-men. And it was made all the more difficult by the tangle of vines and limbs that tore at their clothes and equipment.

The ARVN scout suddenly stopped and held up his fist signaling the rest to hold their positions. The squad leader cautiously crawled up to the scout who, with hand gestures, established that there was the slight odor of smoke which had alarmed the ARVN. Signaling the squad to spread out and move forward, slowly, the Sergeant clicked off the safety of his M-16. Everyone else followed suit and pushed their weapons ahead of them as they crept silently forward.

A sharp crack off to the right announced contact but no one could be sure if it was an M-16 or an AK-47 they had heard. Everyone froze and waited for the Sergeant's signal to proceed. A.J. and Ding-a-Ling slowly maneuvered their cameras into shooting position while still keeping their weapons at the ready. As Ding-a-Ling's Arriflex made a low whirring sound it seemed to trigger more firing up ahead. The Sergeant signaled the squad to split and try to flank the shooter(s) from each side.

A.J. whispered to Ding-a-Ling, *"I'm going with these Marines to the right. You stay with the others and be sure to keep low. See ya' later."*

Ding-a-Ling didn't much like having to remain behind, but, more firing up ahead, made him realize his position was just as vulnerable as on the left or the right. He continued to shoot short bursts with his Arriflex, trying to film the reactions of the Marines nearby. So far no one had sighted the enemy or could determine from where he was firing.

Suddenly, one of the Marines on the right cried out, "I'm hit! Sarge, I'm hit!

A.J., who was the closest to the injured man, tried to crawl to him to assist but the Marine said in a hoarse whisper—*"Keep back, Big Guy. He's got me zeroed in and is just waiting for you to show yourself so he can pick you off, too. I'm not hit bad, just a crease in my thigh. I'll play 'dead' until the Sarge locates him and 'dusts'*

him. The ARVN say's he thinks there's 2 or 3 snipers up in the trees.
They'd rush us if there were more."

Three quick bursts of M-16 automatic fire indicated the Marines had found at least one VC. The firing was followed by the crashing of brush and the 'thump' of a falling body.

"He got that one," the wounded Marine whispered.

The Sergeant waved Ding-a-Ling and the two marines on the left to move up.

"I count two more in those trees to the left. Cover me while I try to get up under them where I can get a clear shot."

"Sarge, let me go. I've got this BAR (Browning Automatic Rifle) *and I can cut the trees right out from under them. I just need a little opening."* whispered a young PFC. *"OK, you got it, Jimmy. 'Dust' 'em good!"*

An instant later, the jungle silence was shattered by the thunder of the BAR cutting loose on full automatic. The other two snipers dropped like rocks, kicked a few times, and lay still.

"I've checked around, Sergeant, and I think we've cleaned out all the VC around here," the ARVN Scout informed the squad leader. "I think they were put in here only to harass us, and to keep us away from the villagers."

"OK, then, you 'Lean-Mean Jungle Fighters'. Let's dee dee mau for camp and report this contact. This should keep us off patrol-duty for 1 or 2 days,—but don't count on it!"

"Oh, Hell," A.J. cursed. "I didn't even get to fire a shot!"

"Oh, but, we sure got some fine pictures," Ding-a-Ling reminded him.

"Collins, can you walk?"

"Yeah, Sarge. The bullet hit my canteen, ricocheted around and only dug a small chunk out of my hip. I'm still 'mobile.'"

"Let's get a dressing on it, then, and a couple of you grunts give him a hand.

We're movin' out. Now!"

The patrol moved into line and worked their way through the jungle without further contact. In minutes they picked up the trail and cautiously hurried for 'home'; alert for 'boobie' traps and snares that might have been set since their earlier passing.

A.J. and Ding-a-Ling were greeted by Senior Chief Brady as they dropped their gear on their cots.

"Clean yourselves up. Then get all your data sheets and film together so we can get it on the next courier flight, stateside. I want the whole team to muster in the mess tent for de-briefing in an hour. We have orders to return to Saigon, chop, chop."

"Chief, we'll need a few minutes to get names and hometowns of the Marines on the patrol. See if we can commandeer a typewriter in the Admin tent and we'll have this stuff ready in jig-time."

"Fine, A.J.. Ding-a-Ling's our 'college boy' so have him do the typing. It'll go faster."

"Yeah," Mad Man piped up, "A.J.'s 'D.C. secretary' typing method'll take all afternoon."

"Whadya mean, Mad Man, 'D.C. secretary' method?"

"You know, 'Huntin' Pecker.'"

"Enough of that, now. We've got a lot to do before we can haul our asses back south," Brady said.

The team gathered in the mess tent, and, while they gobbled some sandwiches and Cokes, Chief Brady quizzed A.J. and Ding-a-Ling, and wrote up his report.

"While you two were playing 'Ernie Pyle' in the jungle I got a phone call from 7th fleet Detachment 'Charlie' that we're to meet up with our new Detachment OinC (Officer in Charge) sent to coordinate our ops from Saigon."

"Chief, you said 'our new detachment OinC' is in Saigon. What's the deal?"

Mad Man asked.

"I didn't get a chance to ask 'who', but, San Diego decided the Far East Detachment OinC should be closer to what's happening. Yokosuka is just too far away for him to control the Vietnam operation and they aren't too happy to have us under 7th Fleet control. Things can happen too damn fast for word to go from Saigon to Yokosuka and back.

"I also have some good news for you guys. No more living in the Mai Khan while we're in Saigon. Whoever the new OinC is, he sweet talked the billeting officer of ComNavForV into letting him rent a four-bedroom villa for the CCG detachment."

"Who's paying for it, Chief?" Caesar inquired.

"We all are. It'll be run like a co-op. We each pay a part of our per diem, pro-rated for each day we're in town. It sure will beat trying to catch a hotel room when we arrive late in the evening. It'll also give us a place where we can keep all our gear secure. And, besides, Saigon is filling up and rooms are getting more expensive and scarcer than hen's teeth."

"Sounds great to us, Senior Chief!" said Caesar. "By the way, I'll need to know all you guys' pants and shoe sizes. I've made a little cumshaw deal with the 3rd's supply Sergeant. He's going to slip us some real jungle fatigues and combat boots before we leave."

"Fine, Caesar. Just what do we do in exchange?—or, maybe I shouldn't ask?"

Brady remarked.

"Nothin' to it, Chief!" Caesar came back, "He's got hisself a new Nikon and I said we'd fix him up with a dozen rolls of Kodachrome."

"Fair enough. But keep it quiet. No need for anyone else to know."

"Mum's the word, Senior Chief!"

When the team packed to return to Saigon, they had four additional boxes to load on the plane.

"The Sergeant told me we'd probably need more than one change of clothes, and, they'd be easier to account for if we took the stuff while it's still in the packing boxes. He said the Vietnamese dock workers are always 'losing' boxes of stuff between the ship and the warehouse, anyway," Caesar explained.

"These boxes say we must have enough here to provide for the <u>whole CCG Far East Detachment</u>, Little Caesar!" Chief Brady marveled.

"Just a little 'Chicago fringe benefit', Chief."

FIVE

Arriving at Tan Son Nhut Airport, the photo team was confronted with a new development. As they disembarked from the Air Force C-130 and entered the terminal, they encountered a sea of people and luggage between them and the Navy Liaison desk.

"What the bloomin' Hades is happening here, Sailor?" Senior Chief Brady asked, when he was finally able to squeeze up to the counter. It was a struggle, getting the attention of the Navy Petty Officer and to make himself heard above the buzz of the crowd.

"Are these people coming or going?"

"They're all coming in, Senior Chief," he replied. "We get 20 to 30 aircraft a day bringing in more troops, Civil Service workers, medics, and civilian contractors. In addition to all that they're transporting refugees looking for a safe haven in the 'big city', trying to escape the war in in the 'boonies.'"

"This is worse that Times Square on New Years Eve!" said A.J..

"I ain't seen this much humanity since I got caught in an 'Amway' convention back in Vegas," added Mad Man.

"They ain't this many people in all of Hog Switch Holler," Redneck added his evaluation of the situation.

"Can you get me a line to the 7th Fleet Detachment Office in The Rex Hotel?" Brady asked. "We need transportation for six men and about 600 pounds of gear."

He was handed a phone and given the number to call, and then, left to his own devices. The sailor had to get back to his duties as 'ring-master' of the growing circus in front of him.

It was an hour later when a truck finally arrived and the driver was able to locate the team.

They quickly discovered that their wild ride into Saigon a few weeks before, was tame compared to the traffic snarl they had to navigate on this trip. Their driver was obviously a student of the '30s racecar driver Barney Oldfield, though, because he flew in and out of the congestion like he was on the back straight-away at Indianapolis.

"I don't see how you can remain so calm, cool, and collected, having to deal with this mess," said A.J.

"Like the tourist in New York was told when he asked how to get to Carnegie Hall—'Practice, Man, practice'!" Mad Man replied.

"When are you going to get some new jokes, '<u>Man</u>'?" Caesar asked.

The driver pulled up to the curb in front of one of the row-houses near downtown Saigon.

"Here you are, Guys. Welcome back to 'Psycho City.'"

The house was what would be a three-story condo in LA or Chicago, but, in previously French Saigon, it was referred to as a 'Villa'. It set back from the street behind a high corrugated-metal wall, topped with barbed-wire.

The men turned-to unloading their gear and piled it on the sidewalk. A.J. let out a piercing whistle to attract someone inside to come open the gate for them and they were soon greeted by a tall, lanky sailor in T-shirt and shorts.

"Welcome to Headquarters, CCG Det. Alpha One. We've been expecting you. I'm George Kutter, they call me 'Teach.'"

"Glad to meet you Teach. I'm Senior Chief Brady, and the rest of these mugs can introduce themselves when we get this stuff inside."

"These are some 'digs,'" Ding-a-Ling remarked. "You sure you got room for all of us?"

"Lordy, yes. We got four bedrooms with two, three-level bunk beds in each one. Plus we also got three or four fold-up cots we can break out if that ain't enough," Teach assured them.

Inside the villa, they were welcomed by the OinC of Det. Alpha.

"Hi, Senior Chief! Long time no see!" The Officer shouted as Brady and his gang trooped into the living room.

"I'll be a sumbitch!" Brady laughed. "They didn't tell me <u>you</u> were our new OinC! Fellas, I want you to meet an old buddy of mine, Harv—scratch that—<u>Ensign</u> Harvey Duncan. We worked together about four years ago, back at the Naval Photo Center, in DC."

"Tell the truth, now, Senior Chief. I worked for YOU! He was a 'Boot Chief' and I was a lowly Second Class Photo-Mate. He's the cause of my being in this uniform!

Without him riding me to study, I probably wouldn't have made First. But, that wasn't enough. After I made it, he had to keep on my ass until I put in for LDO (Limited Duty Officer). He was like a puppy dog, nippin' at my heels 'til I got selected for commission."

"And I was more proud of you getting that gold bar on your collar, Sir, than I was when I got the star over my anchor device.

"Now, I know how we made out with getting this villa to crash in! Guys, he was never afraid of the 'brass' and could argue his case better than any 'Philadelphia Lawyer' you'll ever run across. Our job just got a helluva' lot less complicated. I kid you not, this man will always go to bat for us—just don't screw up, though, cause he's no push-over if you need taken down a peg. It's sure great to see you, again, ENSIGN!"

"Same to ya', Buster."

"Is that what they call you, Senior Chief?" Mad Man asked.

"Only my folks and Mr. Duncan call me that! To you I'm still Senior Chief Brady!" he laughed.

"Gottcha' Bus . . . , oops, I mean Senior Chief."

"Men, This here studious-looking geek is Storekeeper Third Class George Kutter. We call him 'Teacher' for short, like the character in the TV show 'Welcome Back Kotter,'" said Ensign Duncan. "I picked him up in Yokosuka, he's got the thankless job of 'bookkeeper' and billeting coordinator for this whole shebang. He'll set you up with your bunk assignments and clue you in on how the villa will operate."

"Hi, guys. While I have you all here, I'd like to explain our cash-flow system, then I'll get you stabled. First off, we have a 'buy-in' charge of $100 each. That's to set up a reserve in case we have too many of you out in the field in any one month. Your rent will be pro-rated for the number of days you spend in Saigon, payable on the first payday following. So, you see, the 'reserve' is to cover the villa rent so we don't come up short.

We also have to pay a maid we hired through Support HQ Civilian Employee Pool. She gets paid $1.50 a day, for house cleaning and laundry—only the light stuff, scivies, socks, etc. You'll have to scrub you own fatigues, civies and uniforms.—Or you can take them to the Chinese laundry down the street. They do a good job of starching and pressing, and it's well worth the few piastres they charge. Any questions?"

"Sounds fine with us," said Brady, "I don't think any of our gang can kick about not having to sleep in some 'flea bag' hotel, where even the cockroaches check out after they take one look. We've had our fill of that."

All went well with Brady's men settling in and getting to relax for a while. That first evening they all went out together to a restaurant nearby that Ensign Duncan and Teacher had discovered.

"It's called the 'Victory Restaurant,'" Teach told them. "Victory over what I don't know, but they serve authentic Chinese food on white tablecloths, and the prices are great. When we first started going there, the clientele was almost all Chinese business—men. Now, it's about 50-50, Chinese and 'round-eyes'. We were steered to it by the real estate lady who found us this villa. She's really been a great help to us, cutting the red-tape and fixing up the place. She even sent over some Vietnamese workmen to help us set up the bunk-beds and move in the furniture," he said.

"She was educated in the States so she speaks English better than Red Neck—which isn't saying that much. She's also good looking, but hands <u>off</u>! We don't screw up a good thing when we have it."

As they waited for their meal to be served, Chief Brady said, "That brings to mind something the OinC told me. You guys are <u>not</u>, and I emphasize <u>NOT</u> to bring any women friends to the villa! One of the strongest stipulations laid down by ComNavForV, in granting us permission to live on the local economy, was that this was not going to become a 'Snake Ranch'—His words! We mess up and it's back to hotels! Understood?"

"Understood, Senior Chief," A.J. said. "We know better than to blow this 'cushy' deal."

The meal was, as promised, very tasty and very reasonable. On Ensign Duncan's suggestion, each man had ordered a different entré and then they all shared, family style.

"Senior Chief, I'm glad nobody ordered dove. Your little tale about that one has made me very cautious about biting into anything that I haven't inspected carefully, and studied on, a bit," Ding-a-Ling said.

Teacher was enlighten to Brady's Korean epicurean experience to the accompaniment of groans and gagging sounds from all around the table. A couple bottles of rice wine, shared around the table, topped off the meal and left everyone in a mellow mood.

"Whooee! Them was some good vittles!" Red Neck said. "Ah don't know what half of the stuff was, and I don't think I want to know, but I'm as full as a tick on my ol' 'coon dog Duke's ass-end."

Some of the men decided to stop off and have a few drinks at Mimi's Bar. Ensign Duncan, and the rest proceeded to walk back to the villa. On their way they passed through the Market Square where, off to one side, stood four wooden poles backed by a wall of sand bags. Just months earlier this had served as the public execution locale. The spectacle had been discontinued but the poles had been left in place as a reminder to all, the consequences of opposing the power-in-charge of 'democratic' South Vietnam.

"I get chills up my spine every time I pass by here," Ensign Duncan remarked. "To think, dozens of living beings could be tied up there, then shot dead,—for everyone to witness, including women and little children."

"'War is Hell', Sir."

"Trite, but true, Teach."

As they drew near the villa, they saw an MP Jeep parked in front. In the Jeep were two MPs and a Navy Lieutenant Junior Grade, who, on seeing them approach, got out and asked: "Are you Ensign Harvey Duncan?"

"That's right, Sir."

"I'll need to see your ID, please."

"What's this all about, Lt.?" Senior Chief Brady asked.

"I have a highly classified message for you Ensign, and my orders are to be damn sure I give it to you, and <u>only you</u>. Don't open it until you're inside, alone, and away from any windows."

"Aye, aye, Sir," Duncan replied.

His mission completed, the Ltjg. got back in the Jeep and they drove off. The Ensign and his group quickly entered the villa and he immediately went off to the third-floor bedroom he and Senior Chief Brady shared. A few minutes later he came down to the living room and joined his curiosity-filled men. In hushed tones, he told them: *I want everyone to muster here at 0630 in the morning. Have your cameras checked and loaded, and carry only what personal stuff you'll need for two days.*

Weapons won't be needed—in fact, they're forbidden! I'll tell you the job when we're all together here in the morning. It's top hush, hush, so don't anyone leave the villa tonight."

"Gotcha, Sir," Chief Brady answered, "Now, turn in and get some zzzee's, fellas. I got a feeling you'll need to be bright-eyed and bushy-tailed at 0630."

Fortunately, the men who stopped off at 'Mimi's', returned fairly early and reasonably sober. The Senior Chief passed the Ensign's orders on to them and everyone hit the sack. Only the 'party animals' were able to sleep much. The tension and excitement had the rest too keyed-up to relax.

At 0600, everyone was gathered in the living room, eagerly anticipating Ensign Duncan's news. Each man had his gear packed, ready to roll.

"Hey Chief, I think we should name this villa, 'The House of the Rising Sun', like in the song," Mad Man said.

"Where'd you get that idea," Ding-a-Ling asked.

"Well, when the sun came up this morning, it was hitting me full in the face. It about blinded me. I had to hang my poncho over the window to tone it down.".

"Yeah," Redneck added. "That's the song's about a N'awleans Cat House. I don't know if ComNavForV will like it if he gets wind of it. You know what his reservations were when we got this villa."

The discussion was halted, when Mr. Duncan strolled into the room. His mood very serious and intense.

"OK. Whatever you say, Mad Man." Ensign Duncan said. "Now, I see you're all anxious to find out what's going on. So, I'll get right to it. The reason for all the secrecy, Secretary of Defense McNamara is arriving at 1100 today for an inspection tour. The VC and ChiComs would like nothing better than to get him in their sights. This info is for CCG ears <u>only</u>. This means y'all keep your lips buttoned.

"We've been assigned to document his travels in-country, so we've got to look sharp and <u>be</u> sharp.

"The Senior Chief, and I will accompany the Secretary aboard his plane. A.J., you'll take Mad Man, and go out to the Army helo-pad. They'll have a Huey UH-1 standing by to haul you down to the Mekong Delta. You'll follow him on his two or three stops down there. Ding-a-Ling, Red Neck, and Caesar, you'll catch the Da Nang shuttle flight at noon and stand by for his arrival up there in the morning. McNamara's going to visit Chu Lai, Hue, and Quang Tri, so arrange with the Marine Air Wing for a helo to set you down in those places ahead of him. Brady, and I, will try to stay with his party on those stops. But you guys need to be on standby in case we can't crowd in one of their helos. Caesar, you're in charge of the Da Nang ops. Here's all the paperwork you'll need to commandeer whatever transportation necessary. There'll be two DOD photogs and one from CinCPacFlt (Commander in Charge of the Pacific Fleet), riding with the Secretary's party so don't get in their way. But don't let them crowd you out. That's an old D.C. press corps trick. We're all in the same ball club with the same jobs to do. Be forceful, <u>but</u> tactful!" he warned.

"Teach, I'm sorry, but we're going to need you to stay at the villa. We've got a new maid coming in today, and someone needs to be here to get her straight on her duties. She's to come in at noon and leave at 5 PM. She cleans the villa and does the laundry—<u>No</u> <u>cooking</u>! We'll do whatever cooking is done. And don't let her bring in any baskets or bags! It seems, our previous 'Mama San' was picked up yesterday on her way back to the villa. She was carrying three grenades in her basket, under our clean laundry. I shudder to think what she intended to do with them."

"I'd say they're a bit of overkill for rat exterminating," Brady said, "I think she probably had something bigger in mind."

"Holy, Moly!" yelped Red Neck, "Here I thought she kinda reminded me of my Gramma!—Come to think, maybe they ain't so different. My Gramma was a pretty good shot with her ol' 12 gauge. I remember, one night she put a load of bird-shot in the asses of a couple young bucks sniffin' 'round my sis."

"It just goes to show, Guys, you better keep your eyes and ears fine-tuned—even in the villa," said Ensign Duncan. "You can't tell a Commie from a good guy, these days.

They're even in our colleges at home, trying to convert our kids!"

Everyone had their orders and, after a cold breakfast, were given what paper-authority they needed., then gathered up their gear and headed out the door. They were picked up in front of the villa by a sailor in a Navy van with a MACV tag. He drove them to Tan Son Nhut where they separated and proceeded to go their assigned ways.

Ensign Duncan, and Senior Chief Brady, stood by at the terminal, awaiting Secretary McNamara's plane, which was due in 45 minutes. They scouted the area for the best vantage points from which to photograph his arrival.

"Brady, you get over to the left so you'll be shooting with the sun over your shoulder, and I'll try to shoot from directly ahead . . ."

Suddenly, they were surrounded by five, clean-cut Americans in suits, all sporting hearing aids stuck in their ears. Realizing who they were and what he'd just said, Ensign Duncan had to quickly explain the term 'shoot' in photographic terms, and to identify himself and Brady. The 'undercover' security men were finally convinced and allowed the photographers to go on with their work.

"<u>Don't</u>, and I mean, <u>DON'T</u> <u>EVER</u>, use that word around here, if you don't want to wind up in 'cuffs," the apparent leader of the 'suits' admonished.

The arrival went well, with all the VIPs present, including South Vietnam's Vice President Nguyen Cao Ky and Major General Duong Van "Big Minh", (overall commander of the Army of the Republic of Vietnam), greeting the Secretary with handshakes all around. Ambassador Lodge ushered SecDef McNamara to the VIP lounge in the terminal, for some cool refreshments before continuing the tour.

The teams were kept busy during his two-day visit 'in-country' with only one mishap. Brady was doing the still photography, and decided he was OK with the high speed of his TRI-X film, but his Kodachrome would require some extra light in the plane's cabin. To solve the problem, he stuffed a mini-flash-gun and a twelve-pack of M-3 flashbulbs in one of the cargo pockets of his fatigue pants. During the takeoff from Tan Son Nhut, he experienced a very warm sensation on his thigh, and smelled the odor of scorched cloth.

On a quick examination, he discovered all of his flashbulbs had been fired off by the ground radar as the plane passed overhead. Only the heavy starch in his trousers prevented them from catching fire, and saved him a few blisters. No <u>color</u> photos were taken on that flight but everyone got a good laugh, watching the Senior Chief dancing in the aisle, "like a Sioux medicine man," as described by Ensign Duncan.

For a job 'well done', Ensign Duncan told everyone to 'stand down' for a couple of days to get their cameras cleaned and take care of personal business.

"And don't forget to take time to write home," he told them.

SIX

DURING THE 'DOWN time', the Ensign was 'wheeling and dealing' and establishing contacts at the Rex Hotel Officers' Mess. His friendship with the Officer-In-Charge of the ComNavForV motor pool, resulted in getting an 8-passenger stretch van assigned, on permanent custody, to the CCG Detachment (at least for the 'duration'). He was also able to talk the 7th Fleet Detachment Commander into establishing an office on board Tan Son Nhut Airbase, and sharing a couple of rooms with CCG. This gave the teams a base of operations closer to air transportation, as well as a more secure place to store their valuable camera equipment.

"I told you guys Mr. Duncan was a 'standup' officer, didn't I?" Senior Chief Brady asked when he learned what the Ensign had accomplished. "Now we can stop operating like a bunch of gypsies."

"Yeah, Senior Chief." said Teach. "You know what the guys over at Naval Support HQ are saying?—'C C G *stands for 'Crazy Camera Guys'. They don't operate like the rest of the Navy. They're more like McHale's Navy. They don't follow any rules'.*"While the rest of you were hop-scotching all over 'Nam, I spent a lot of hours setting up a supply system with the guys at Support, and fixing up an uncomplicated way we can draw our pay. So, <u>please</u>, you guys, don't fuck it up cutting <u>too</u> many corners, OK?"

"Sure thing, Teach," replied A.J. "I'll make it my job to see they don't."

"Good luck, A.J. You'll need the patience of Job to carry that off," Brady said.

"No, Senior Chief. Just a handfull of knuckles! That ought to be all the 'convincing' any of these yayhoos should need."

"He's made a believer out of me, Senior Chief," said Mad Man.

"Well, I got something to keep you guys out of mischief today, Mad Man. How about you, Caesar, and Ding-a-Ling come along with me. We need to inventory all our camera gear, and move it out to our new Tan Son Nhut office. Now that we have a secure place to stow it, we won't need to keep a duty watch on the villa all the time."

The men turned-to and in no time had everything counted and loaded on the van. Senior Chief Brady took over the driving chore, but not without a word of caution from Ensign Duncan:

"I put my ass on the line for that van, Fellas, so the first one who puts a ding in it, had better know body repair work or <u>his</u> body is going to need some repair!"

While they were busy assembling shelves and stowing the equipment, they were visited by the Warrant Officer in charge of the 7th Fleet Detachment admin staff.

"Thought I'd drop over and see if you need anything in the way of desks and chairs, etc. The Navy Supply department has a warehouse full of all kinds of office equipment, ours just for the asking."

"We sure could use a couple of desks, typewriters, file cabinets and stuff like that," Brady replied.

"Just make out a list and I'll have our storekeeper fill out the chits for Ensign Duncan's signature. We can have this place up and operational by tomorrow afternoon."

"Thanks, a lot, Sir."

"Oh, by the way, the other reason I came over. Our bunch is getting together a beer party for Saturday, and you're all welcome to join us. We're pitching in $5 apiece for the beer and the eats and we've reserved a park on the river west of Saigon. We'll have a real ol' fashioned family picnic."

"Count us in. Sir, and I'm sure some of the others would enjoy some R & R, too. Is the park in a secure area, or should we bring along our artillery to keep the VC from crashing the party?"

"It's as secure as any place in-country can be, so bring your weapons . . . , but we'll hope we don't have to break 'em out. I'll check with you tomorrow for a CCG head count."

"Great. We'll see you then, Sir."

The equipment was all locked up and the office area swept and swabbed so they piled into the van and headed back to the villa to spread the news of the beer party. It was a slow bumper-to-bumper drive from Tan Son Nhut to the villa.

Everyone in Vietnam seemed to be going to town at the same time. The already usual heavy congestion, was even more so.

They had gone only a few blocks, when they heard sirens coming up from the rear. All the traffic pulled to the side to make way for two Jeeps, with MPs manning .30 caliber machine guns, leading a black sedan through the cleared passage.

"Must be only some ARVN colonel," Mad Man commented. "It's only a Chevy,

Chief. If he was anyone important, he'd be riding in a Mercedes or Cadillac, at least."

"Whatever, Mad Man. I've got an idea, so you birds hang on to your perches. I'm going to expedite this trip. We're going home via the expressway!"

As the Senior Chief finished saying that, the follow-up Jeep, on the tail of the VIP caravan, passed them. Brady immediately cut the wheel sharply to the left, turned on his emergency blinkers, gunned the motor, and fell in line behind the Jeep. The MP gave him a quizzical look and the Chief saluted him. The MP laughed and relaxed his grip on the machine gun.

Breezing along at a speed few people had ever driven in the city of Saigon (25 to 30 mph), they quickly reached the street on which the villa was situated. Brady made a sharp right turn, leaving the caravan to go on without them, immediately slowing to a more cautious pace.

"Whoop-tee-do, Chief!" Caesar exclaimed. "That was sure some kinda' dare-devil driving. It's a good thing Mr. Duncan wasn't along. He'd a' had a shit hemorrhage! You're damn lucky you didn't mess up his little 'play-toy'!"

"He may not have, but I sure 'messed up' something," said Ding-a-Ling. "I gotta' wash out my skivvies, again, when we get home!"

"I swear, Little Buddy, I think you got a faulty drain plug!" laughed Mad Man.

"'Luck' had nothing to do with that drivin', Caesar." Brady laughed. "That was pure <u>driving</u> <u>talent</u>! Now, how's about opening the gate so we can put 'Baby' away for the night? And, I suggest we don't say anything to Mr. Duncan about our little 'escort' run. No need to worry the poor man. He has enough to stew about with the normal day's events."

The news about the beer party was greeted with excitement all around. Only Ensign Duncan, Teach, and Ding-a-Ling begged off. Mr. Duncan and Teach had official business to attend to at HQ Support Activities; and Ding-a-Ling was suffering from the 'Saigon Trots' and didn't dare stray too far from the head.

"It'll just be that much more beer and grub for the rest of us," gloated Red Neck.

The following two days passed with routine monotony of general equipment maintenance and small chores, but, finally Saturday arrived. The 'party boys' loaded into the van and followed the Warrant Officer's directions to a pleasant little park on the bank of the upper Saigon River.

"Hey. This makes me recollect our little park, down by the crick, in my hometown o' Hog Switch, Geo'ga," Red Neck said.

The 7th Fleet advance party had the coals white-hot and were starting to lay on some huge mouth-watering T-bones.

"You camera jockeys are just in time. Grab yourselves a beer from one of those coolers over there, and let's get this party to percolatin.'"

The steaks were soon ready, and everyone lined up, 'mess hall style,'—metal trays and all, and began loading up their trays with steaks, beans and salad and all the trimmings.

"Ah've eaten a lot of meals off these trays, but I'll guaran-damn-tee you, they weren't none of 'em tasted as scrumptious as this." Red Neck marveled. "Ah sure hope you got plenty of these here steaks, 'cause Ahm comin' back fo' seconds, and maybe, even thu'ds."

"Red Neck, we have plenty of 'them thar' steaks," the 7th Fleet storekeeper teased him. "We kinda 'liberated' two cases of them off a refrigerator ship yesterday. We traded the crew some 'war relics' that had been stored in a warehouse on the base. A bunch of old Russian and ChiCom rifles that were rendered useless with the touch of a welding rod to the firing chamber, along with parts of some old NVA uniforms taken off North Vietnamese prisoners. They were so tickled to get that junk I swear we mighta' had us the whole ship, if we'd wanted it!"

When everyone (including Red Neck) had had their fill, someone suggested some touch football to work it off.

The game was going well, with excitement running high, when, as usual, something had to spoil it! The afternoon monsoon rains cut loose and turned the football field into a big mud hole. The gang was undaunted though. What was a little rain and mud when you're full of good food and BEER, so the game continued. The uniform of the day quickly became shorts, or swim trunks, with a generous layer of mud from head to foot.

The afternoon grew shorter and it came time to pack up and go back to town. Each man took turns standing under the roof drains, letting the monsoon rain rinse off most of the thick mud. They climbed aboard the vehicles looking like drowned rats but they were laughing and happy. It had been a great day. A day when everyone forgot why they were in this strange, foreign land, half-way around the world from Sanity.

"Senior Chief, we ought to get some steaks and wieners and such, and throw a party at the villa, to return the favor."

"That's a nice thought, Caesar, but I can just see us trying to cook enough steaks, 'and such', for that many men, on our little 2-burner Coleman stove."

"Hey, no sweat! I know where there's one of those 50-gallon oil drums someone has cut in half, put legs on it, and made a great barbecue stove out of it. Nobody is using it and it would sure look nice in our open-air kitchen," Little Caesar came back, enthusiastically.

"You sure nobody's using it?" asked A.J..

"Hell, yeah, I'm sure. It's just sittin' there. Let's go 'liberate' it, Senior Chief!"

"OK, We'll drop the rest of the guys off at the villa, and you and A.J. come along. We'll check this out. You just might have hit on a good plan, Caesar!"

With Caesar calling the turns and Senior Chief Brady at the wheel, the barbecue 'rescue' party took off. Caesar called one last "right turn" and Brady found he was guiding the van into the compound of COMUSMACV (General Westmoreland's

HQ). He was surprised when they received a wave-on, from the MP gate guard, to proceed.

"Did you see that?" asked A.J. "He let us waltz right in without a pause! We're muddy, wet, and out of uniform, and he didn't even have us slow down for an ID check. He must think we're some of them CIA 'spooks'!"

"Stop right here, Chief," Caesar ordered. "We'll just be a minute. Come on, A.J.."

"You guys get the barbecue, while I make a run to the head (restroom). I've gotta' drain some of this beer out of my crankcase or I'll pop a valve. I'll meet you back here in five minutes. We don't need to hang around here too long. This just could get 'hairy'.

I don't like the feelings I'm feeling. The hair is standing up on the back of my neck"

"Aye, aye, Chief," they both replied, in unison.

Five minutes later, Brady returned to the van to find they had unlatched the middle seat, and moved it back to make room for the oil-drum barbecue. A.J. and Caesar were proudly seated in their seat behind the drum, looking like two Buddha statues, their arms crossed over their chests, and with enigmatic smiles on their still-muddy faces.

"I still have a bad feeling about this. If you're ready, let's vamoose!"

"Right, Chief. Let's vamoose!" Caesar repeated.

There was too little room in the driveway to turn the van around, so Brady had to back out of the gate. The MP not only waved them out, he stepped into the street and halted traffic to ensure their safe exit.

"That stupid Sombitch still doesn't have a clue," said A.J. "We could be kidnapping the General and he'd still make like a small-town traffic cop. Talk about your lax security!"

Once out of the gate, and turned towards home, Chief Brady made like a jack rabbit heading for his hole. As the van approached the villa, he hollered over his shoulder to ask, "Caesar, how come this barbecue was just sitting there and no one ever used it?"

"Well, <u>hardly</u> ever, Chief. Once in a while they fired it up, but only to burn some of their classified documents."

"BURN THEIR CLASSIFIED DOCUMENTS??!! Good God, Caesar, you could have got us all shot if that MP hadn't had his head up his 'six'!! All those ashes in that thing are MILITARY HUSH—HUSH secrets. We're going to have to keep this strictly top-secret between the three of us. If anyone ever learns we stole Westmoreland's <u>classified</u> <u>incinerator</u>, we'll all be spending our old age in the Naval Brig at Portsmouth! So, ZIP IT UP!!"

The 'barbecue' was welcomed to its' new home, and, whenever any friends from the COMUSMACV PAO Office visited the villa, the three 'liberators' made it a point to keep them in the living room and <u>away</u> from the kitchen!

SEVEN

Monday morning, following the MACV Barbeque Caper, it's back to the war.

At muster, Ensign Duncan laid out the new assignments for the crews.

"Senior Chief Brady, CINCPAC (Commander Pacific Fleet), wants some coverage of the Seabees operating up in the Highlands. They're working with the Vietnamese up there trying to repair the hydro-electric power plant the VC keep sabotaging. It supplies most of the Central-South Vietnam provinces with electricity—that's why we have those rotating 'brown-outs' in Saigon.

"The CBs have a detachment based about 12 clicks (kilometers) west of Da Lat so we'll fly you in to the strip there and they'll pick you up and take you to their camp. They've been involved almost daily with skirmishes with the VC, so, along with the Nungs, a local Montagnard tribe that Special Forces have recruited and trained, they do almost as much fighting as they do fixing."

"Hot Dog! Does that mean we'll get to see some action, Mr. Duncan?"

"Yeah, Mad Man, you'll probably see all the 'action' you'll ever want, before you get back! Just be sure you all <u>get back!</u> We don't need any of you 'hot shots' going home in a body bag or with parts missing! Don't forget, you're there to take pix and write the stories of <u>their</u> action-packed lives. You'll have as much protection as they can provide, so keep your eye on the viewfinder and you asses <u>down</u>—unless it gets too hot and heavy. Then you have my permission to use whatever weapons you have to save your sorry butts!"

The men all stirred uneasily upon hearing this and a serious cloud moved over them.

"Brady, we've arranged for your team to catch an Air America C-45 that'll be departing at 1100 from the west end of the Tan Son Nhut strip. Take your guys and get all the gear together that you'll need for about a week and be there waiting, when the plane taxis out. They won't wait.

"You've probably all heard that 'Air America' is the CIA's 'secret' little airline, and these guys are a 'hot-to-trot' bunch. They're <u>almost</u> as unorthodox as you yardbirds, so play it 'cool' around them. They know their business!" Ensign Duncan warned the men.

"Teach, I guess we're elected to hold down the villa and keep the home-fires burning 'til the boys come marching home."

"Senior Chief, I've got so much paper work to catch up on, that I'll gladly add it to those 'home-fires.'"

"Yeah, right. OK Guys, Good Luck, and Good Hunting."

With their instructions laid out for them, the men set-to making their preparations.

Excitement was running high, but the usual idle banter was at a minimum. Every one was quietly doing his job and concentrating on details. They all were fully aware it was no time for 'horseplay'. One slip-up now, could be disastrous for the whole team.

Even Mad Man felt the seriousness of 'getting it right'—no second chances.

Senior Chief Brady's men were on the tarmac with their gear stacked, waiting, when the Air America Beechcraft taxied up.

"OK, Sailors. All aboard for Jungle Land." yelled the pilot, a dashing figure with a crushed WW II pilot's cap cocked over one eye, and a thin mustache, reminding the men of the 'Smilin' Jack' character of the 'funny papers'.

Ding-a-Ling spoke for the rest when he commented: "This looks like it has the makings of a 1940's Hollywood WW II fly-boy movie!"

"Don't say that so loud, Jerk!" Mad Man warned. "We gotta fly with this character. and we sure don't want to piss him off before we get back on the ground."

"My concern is more—'can this rattle-trap make it to the end of the runway, much less get in the air,'" Redneck nervously remarked.

Getting airborne, the pilot proved himself to be well qualified to operate the ancient craft, and the men soon relaxed for the one-hour hop to Dalat.

A.J. took the seat just behind the co-pilot, and clamped a pair of earphones on his head to listen to the conversation taking place in the cockpit.

It was a smooth flight, in an azure-blue sky, but, arriving over where Dalat should be, they found the mountain tops 'socked in' with low-hanging clouds.

"I'm going to scout around a bit," A.J. heard 'Smilin' Jack' tell the co-pilot.

"Maybe there's an opening in this crap that we can sneak through. Keep your eyes open."

That said, the plane banked sharply to the left and started making 'box-turns' over the general area where Da Lat should be.

The pilot finally announced that it looked like they'd have to return to Tan Son Nhut, and try again, later in the day, when, he suddenly shouted: "I see a hole! Hang on, we're going in for a landing—I hope!"

The photogs all peered anxiously out their windows but none of them saw any 'hole' in the dense overcast.

As the pilot leveled out they broke through the cloud cover and Mad Man shouted, "Hey, I see buildings!"

"I do, too," added Little Caesar, "And we're mighty close. We just passed by a church steeple and it couldn't have been more than 10 or 15 feet below the wing tip!"

The men didn't have long to ponder the path of the plane before it dropped down to a hard landing on the short runway. The wheels had barely touched ground 'til 'Smilin' Jack' hit the brakes and reverse-pitched the props, bringing the plane to a squealing stop only feet from the end of the runway.

"That's what we call: a 'controlled—crash', the pilot cheerily announced from the cockpit. "These little strips were made more for kites, than aircraft," as he swung the plane around, and cut the engines. "Shake a leg and get your gear unloaded. As soon as we get the rest of the cargo out of here, we're back into the 'wide blue yonder'. Next stop, L.A. International! All ashore, what's goin' ashore!"

"Man, you don't have to tell me twice," Little Caesar answered. "I want my feet back on good ole 'Terry-Firmer'—the firmer the better, and the better the sooner!"

True to plan the SeaBees had a 6-by truck waiting for the team and, in minutes, the photo equipment and personal luggage was piled aboard.

"Howdy, Senior Chief, I'm Petty Officer Vicar. We have some supplies to off-load from the plane, so it'll be a few minutes before we head for camp. Might I suggest we hike a couple of blocks over to town and get something to eat. My guys and I missed chow to get here on time and you're probably hungry, too. It'll be at least an hour and a half getting to camp so we'd best chow-down while we can."

"Sounds like a grand idea to me," said A.J. "My bellybutton and my backbone are about to rub calluses on each other if I don't get something to separate them."

"OK, Petty Officer Vicar. First stop, food," directed Brady.

"Aye, Aye, Senior Chief. And make that 'Vic', We CBs, below Chief, are kinda informal out here in the boonies. I'll tell my two riflemen where we're going and they'll join us as soon as our supplies are aboard."

With their hunger satisfied, everybody climbed onto the truck and tried to make themselves comfortable on all the cases and bags. The ride down the hill to camp proved not to be very 'comfortable', however.

"This road used to be black-top, but, with little, or no maintenance, and the heavy monsoon rains, it's so full of pot-holes it rivals the back streets of New York City in the spring," Vic remarked to Brady, who was riding 'shotgun' in the cab with him. "We wear out the shocks and springs on about one vehicle a week."

"This sure ain't doin' my hemorrhoids any good, fellas," Mad Man complained.

"How's about tossing me one of those duffle bags to park my butt on, will ya, Ding-a-Ling?"

The bumpy road turned out not to be the worst part of the trip, however.

As the truck teetered around a sharp bend, there was the sharp 'crack, crack' of rifle fire, and they were showered with a cloud of dirt and debris from a mortar shell explosion on the shoulder of the road where they'd been just a second before.

Both of the CB riflemen sprang into action and poured several bursts of automatic fire into the jungle on both sides of the road. No enemies were visible but it had the effect of making them take cover and brought a pause in their firing.

At the same time, Vic shouted: "Hang on!" as he 'put the pedal to the metal' and began a zig-zag course down the road. The big truck responded like a cat with his tail ablaze, sending the passengers rolling around among the cases and boxes, bruising knees, elbows, and sculls. Maneuvering around several curves in the road, they finally outran the fire zone and Vic relaxed his pressure on the gas pedal.

"Sorry about the 'welcoming party' back there, Guys," he said. "I should have warned you about 'Charlie's' traffic control phobia. They're always poppin' away at us up here. We're lucky to have the help of the Nung villagers. They drive the VC nuts by chasin' them all over these mountains. They keep coming back, but, having to move around so much to avoid the Nung, they're unable to carry any really big weaponry. They're limited to small Chinese mortars, light machine guns and their usual AK-47s."

"WOW!" Mad Man interrupted. "That sure got my mind off my piles in a hurry!"

"Yeah, well I don't got piles," said Little Caesar. "But right now I'm sitting in somethin' mighty soft!"

"You and Ding-a-Ling must have been eating chow off those Le Loi Street ptomaine carts in Saigon. I sure hope you both brought along plenty of skivvies," said A.J. "You'll probably be changing them pretty often up here, from the looks of things."

"Well, let's just hope those guys' skivvies are the only casualties while we're on this mountain." Brady said.

"Chief!" A.J. shouted over the sound of the of the truck's motor. "I think I got some good film back there! I had my camera rolling to record our trip, and when all that shooting started. I was aimed in that direction. I think I caught some of the muzzle flashes. I <u>know</u> I got that mortar blast, 'cause, suddenly, the only thing I could see in the viewfinder was dirt and rocks flying right at me.!"

"Good on ya, A.J. That's what we all should be looking out for. Photograph anything that looks interesting to <u>you</u> and you can bet it'll probably be interesting to the public. That camera is their eyes and your job is to make John Q. Public an on-scene witness."

"I don't know how sharp it'll be, with all that bouncing around, but, I used my old 'knee-action, skiing stance' and held it as steady as I could. CINCPAC should be able to edit out the <u>really</u> shaky stuff."

"What's a 'knee-action, skiing stance', A.J.?"

"That's when I stand with my feet slightly apart and my knees bent, like you do when you ski, Caesar. Then I just kinda' ride with the bumps. It works like the suspension on a car—as a matter of fact, car makers used to call it 'knee action' before some smart ass PR guy put some artsy-fartsy technical name on it."

The lesson was interrupted by Vic announcing: "Camp's just over this rise. We're about home free, this time, fellas."

They had been gently climbing for the past couple of miles and now topped out on a vast plateau.

"This used to be some big shot Indo-Chinese's poppy plantation where he grew opium and got rich," Vic told the men. "But, when the French left, the new South Vietnamese government chased him into Laos or Cambodia. We're using some of his old buildings for our base-camp, but, for the most part, the place had deteriorated into just rubble 'til we 'dozed' it and cleaned it off."

"That big field in front of the camp makes a great clear-fire zone to stop anyone from approaching from the south," Brady observed.

"You bet, Senior Chief. It also makes a neat helo pad. We keep the brush and grass mowed down to remove any cover. On the east and west sides of the camp, shear cliffs drop about 200 feet which not even a monkey could scale. That leaves the north side our only vulnerable spot. But we've cut a road down that side that intersects with the main road from Saigon to the power plant. The Nung Montagnards patrol the whole area real well, and, so far, we haven't had any attacks on the camp from that direction.

"The VC mainly just harass us around the plant and along the trails and roads."

The base consisted of one run-down villa, another old building that might have been a stable or barn, a couple of steel 'Butler Huts', and 6 or 7 hardback tents. The barn and one Butler Hut were being used as a machine shop and garage for the vehicles and heavy construction equipment. The other Butler was the warehouse for the camp supplies and repair parts for the equipment and the power plant. The 'villa' served as office space and the hardbacks were for berthing and a mess hall.

"You've got quite an operation here, Vic."

"We do our best to make it like a home away from home, Senior Chief." chuckled Vic. "All we lack is a mother to tuck us in, but, our LCPO (Leading Chief) say's he draws the line at taking on that job."

The Detachment OinC, along with his Leading Chief came out to welcome the newcomers. Vic made the introductions all around.

"Lieutenant Carson, Senior Chief Holliday, this here's Senior Chief Photographer's Mate Brady and his Combat Camera Group. They're goin' to make us all movin' picher stars."

"Yeah, Vic, we're aware of their mission." the Lt. said. "Glad to meet you Senior Chief. Any way we can be of assistance, just ask. Just so it doesn't interfere with our job. The men have all been briefed. Since Vic, here, is anxious to be in 'pichers' I'm going to assign him as your 'gopher' and liaison, so, anything you need, tell him. How was the ride down 'hell's highway'?"

"Well, Sir, I wouldn't recommend it to anyone with a weak heart or high blood pressure."

"Yeah, Lt." Vic chimed in, "In addition to the washboard ride, Charlie gave us the '21 gun salute' back down the road a piece. 'Old Betsy' about threw a piston gettin' us out of there. But the old gal came through in the pinch, again. No casualties, if you don't count a few bruises and a soiled pair of skivvies," Vic laughed.

"As you can see, some of our guys take a personal pride in their vehicles." the Lt. said. "Some of them, I believe, would take 'em to bed with them if it wasn't already too crowded in the bunkhouse."

"Ha!" Brady chuckled, "My guys are the same way about their cameras. The difference is—their cameras are small enough that they <u>can,</u> and very often <u>do,</u> sleep with them."

Well, Senior Chief, Vic will get you all moved in and we'll see you at chow call this evening. Hope you get all the photos you need and you enjoy your stay with us." Holliday said. "I guess you'll want to get out and get the lay of the land in the morning. I'll put a vehicle at your disposal while you're here and Vic can drive you wherever you say. Again, 'welcome aboard.'"

"Thanks, Holliday, See ya later."

EIGHT

AT 0530 IN the morning the troops were rousted out by the shrill recording of a bugle blasting 'Reveille' over the PA system. Everyone went through their morning ablutions of 'sh . . . , shave, shower, and shine', then fell into formation for muster and the posting of the POD (plan-of-the-day). From there, it was off to the mess tent for a CB-style breakfast.

"Jeez, you guys really eat good!" Redneck marveled. "Last night it was primo roast beef with au jus and all the trimmings, now, this morning—sausage gravy and biscuits, like my Mama makes, plus ham, eggs cooked to order, pancakes and canned fruit. I ain't et this good since I left Gawgia!"

"When you do the kind of rough-neck work we do, you need a hearty meal," Vic responded. "Before we deployed from Port Hueneme, California, the Lt. 'shanghai-ed' the best cook in the Battalion. Between his culinary talents and Lt. Carson's connections with the Supply Officer in charge of unloading the provisions ships, we eat the best in 'Nam."

"Enough bullshit, guys. I've got our day all mapped out and we need to get on our horses."

The five photogs gathered around Senior Chief Brady as he laid out their assignments.

"A.J., I want you, Ding-a-Ling and Mad Man to go with the repair crew down to the power plant. Get all the 'establishing shots' and as much working stuff as you can. I'm going to take Redneck and Caesar and go with the Lt. to the Nung Montagnard village and get acquainted with the 'big Honcho' up there. They're a little superstitious about being photographed. I'm going to have to smooth the way so we'll be able to include them in the story. They play an important part in this project so we need their cooperation."

The trip to the Nung village was over a narrow, mountainous road which, at times, almost disappeared in the dense jungle growth.

"Keep your eyes peeled through here, Senior Chief," admonished Lt. Carson as he steered the Jeep along the almost invisible track. "The Nung Montagnard patrols keep the VC away pretty much, but, sometimes some fanatic will sneak in, just to get one 'pop' at us. That tight vigil and our good luck have kept our casualty rate down to only two men getting minor wounds," He added. "Not serious enough to send them 'down the hill' to the hospital, though. Our two corpsmen patched them up and they were back on the job in a couple days."

"I'd say that's a pretty good record, Lt.," said Little Caesar. "I just hope nothing happens, while we're here, to spoil it."

As the Jeep bounced over a small rise, the jungle gave way to reveal a village, surrounded by 'concertina' wire and overlooked by twenty-foot guard towers at each corner.

They proceeded through the gate, which was flanked by two gun emplacements, and were greeted by a smiling group of Nung children, men and women. The 'jungle telegraph' had announced their coming before they were 2 'clicks' (km) out of the CB compound.

"These people have lived in these jungles all their lives and nothing goes on around here, that they don't know about," the Lt. said.

The Green Beret NCO, who was liaison and 'advisor' to the Nungs, was pleased to see the Jeep also carried a supply of beer and cigarettes for his four-man detachment.

"You're sure a welcome sight, Lt. We're down to drinking Montagnard rice wine and rolling their mountain-grown tobacco, both of which are pretty strong and horrible stuff."

"Knew you'd appreciate this, Sarge. Our truck came back from Nha Trang yesterday, loaded with 'goodies', so we're stocked up with the 'necessities' for a few days.

"This here is Senior Chief Brady of the Combat Camera Group Detachment, and Petty Officers Cessario, and Reddick." Lt. Carson said. "They're taking pictures and doing a story about our little operation up here, and wanted to get some coverage of the Nung Montagnards, too. Can you kinda' smooth the way with their head man?"

"No sweat, Lt. They're usually pretty leery of having their pictures taken, something about 'stealing their soul', but one of my guys brought his Polaroid along and has taken quite a few snaps and passed them around. So, they're sorta loosened up and the superstition has turned to curiosity."

"Hey, Sarge, that's great!" Brady said. "We carry a Polaroid with us, too, to break the ice. That'll be a big help. We'll leave some film with you, since you've already taken care of that for us."

The Sergeant escorted the visitors to the center of the village and introduced them to the Nung leader.

Caesar was already busy photographing the assemblage with his 16mm Arriflex and Redneck had his Nikon, loaded with Kodachrome, and was snapping away, right and left.

The Nung head-man invited the group to sit and partake of the rice wine and then, through the Sergeant, asked Senior Chief Brady to submit to having a small tattoo placed on his shoulder to show his 'brotherhood' with the tribe.

Following the wine and the tattoo ceremony, the entire tribe gathered around the Americans and sang and chanted. The guests were then feted to a meal of steamed jungle vegetables and roasted meat.

"I'm not going to ask what kind of animal this was," Caesar remarked, as he filled his face, "but I've got a sneaking hunch it ain't chicken or beef."

"What we don't know, can't hurt us—I HOPE!" Redneck mumbled, his mouth full.

At the end of the meal, Caesar reported to Brady that he and Redneck had all the background coverage and 'one-shots' (single, head-and-shoulder close-ups) that he needed.

There was much shaking of hands and hugs and the Americans climbed into their Jeep for the trip back, arriving just as dusk was setting in.

"What's with AJ and his guys? Why aren't they back from the power plant yet?"

Brady asked Vic.

"We got a radio call a couple hours ago that they were finished down there and would be heading back shortly, Senior Chief."

A.J., Mad Man, and Ding-a-Ling had wrapped up their photography and were packing up their gear, when, a sudden rattle of small arms fire came pouring in from the trees on the edge of the clearing, where the power plant stood.

"TAKE COVER!!"—And everyone dived for the nearest hole.

From their bunkers the CBs, photographers, Vietnamese laborers and ARVN Security Forces began spraying the tree-line with their M-16s, M-60 machine guns and M-79 Grenade Launchers.

In the bunker with A.J., one little ARVN soldier was hunkered down in the corner with his rifle across his knees.

"Hey, Dink, Get your ass up from there and start shooting!" A.J. yelled at him.

The Vietnamese looked at him with sad eyes and replied:

"Window too high. Me too short. Need Box!"

For the next 30 seconds, or so, A.J. was too taken over with laughter to do much shooting, either.

"HOLD YOUR FIRE!" Senior Chief Holliday yelled. "They've pulled back and the Nungs are rounding up some stragglers for questioning."

On close inspection, they found that the firing was mainly to cover 'sappers', who, in the failing light, were trying to sneak close enough to plant their satchel-charges around the generators.

Among the attackers' casualties, they found a young Vietnamese boy of 12 who, for several weeks, had been a sort of camp mascot and 'gofer'. In a bag, still slung around his shoulder, was an explosive charge meant for the power plant.

"This fucked up war is like none I've ever heard of," Holliday commented. "You can't tell friend from enemy, even with a score card. We were lucky we drove them back before they got those things set," he said, "We'd be weeks repairing what we just got through repairing."

The Nung Montagnards returned with two captives, still weighted down with their demolition packs.

"I managed to get some pix of the action,—between shooting and ducking," Ding-a-Ling said. "It's tough trying to work a camera with one hand, while you're firing with the other, so I don't know if any of it will be worth a shit."

"Hey, man, getting through that without getting your ass shot is worth more than any damn movin' pitchers," Mad Man chuckled.

"Yeah, but that's why we're over here in this jungle hell, and I try to put the pix first."

"Well, don't get too damn 'Gung Ho', Ding," A.J. replied.

The team observed the ARVN Commandos as they interrogated the prisoners, but it soon became too much for them to watch.

As they went back to preparing to leave, Ding-a-Ling asked, "Senior Chief Holliday, how can we let them treat those men so brutally?"

"Well, this is <u>their</u> country, and their ways are very different from ours. We're only here to advise and assist, and we can't interfere with them doing things their way—as much as it goes against our grain."

"Let's load up the truck and head back to camp. We don't want to get ambushed on the road after dark, A.J. advised.

"Amen!" Mad Man agreed.

The driver had just made the turn from the main highway, and was beginning the two-mile climb up to the camp, when he slowed the truck, and, in a whisper, said:

"*Look! Off to your right about fifty yards. There's an Asian Tiger just standing there, watching us. We see one, now and then, but never so close up.*"

"*Pull ahead a couple feet, so I can get a clear shot,*" Ding-a-Ling said.

"*Hey, Sailor! They're protected animals, up here. You ain't supposed to shoot them!!*

"*Don't get excited, Man! I just meant, 'so I could take pictures of him'. The jungle brush was obstructing my view. People back home don't realize there <u>are</u> tigers out here in this Hell-hole.*"

"*Shit,*" the driver said. "*We even got elephants runnin' lose in these jungles. We very seldom see them, though, except way off in the distance. They're extremely shy in the wild,*"

That night, after showering off the road dust, and downing a hearty CB meal, everyone in the camp had some <u>real</u> 'dry-land' 'sea stories' to relate over their cold beers.

NINE

JUST AFTER BREAKFAST, a CH-47 "Chinook" helo landed in the clearing south of the CB camp. Three CBs, with all their field equipment, disembarked and reported in for duty with the Detachment.

Along with the CB passengers, and a load of supplies, the helo crew brought word to Senior Chief Brady to pile his crew and equipment aboard, and return to Saigon for new assignments.

The CBs eagerly unloaded the supplies, and the pilot gave the order: "Senior Chief, get your men aboard, We're not going to stick around here and become the prime target in a 'VC turkey-shoot.'"

The CCG team hurriedly loaded their gear aboard the helo and, while doing it, discovered they had an additional six big, cardboard boxes.

"Where the Hell did this extra cargo come from?" A.J. asked. "We didn't have all these boxes when we got here!"

"Don't get your balls in an uproar, A.J.," Caesar shouted over the noise of the helo revving up. "I asked Vic if he had couple of extra flack jackets, since we hadn't been issued any, yet. So he took me out to the warehouse and loaded his Jeep down with plenty for everybody—and then some.

"He told me Battalion Supply had screwed up and sent them enough for all the CBs in-country. Besides, none of the guys here wear them much. They're too damn hot and heavy for their kind of sweat-labor."

"OK. Load 'em up. What the shit are you going to pick up next, Caesar?"

"Hey. If we can use it, I'll 'liberate' it."

A half hour after setting down, the big 'Shit Hook', as the Chinook was called by the troops, was back in the air and heading southeast for the 'Big City'.

"Damn, I was just gettin' used to that fine CB chow," Little Caesar growsed." I bet we won't eat that good anywhere else in 'Nam."

"Or in ANY Navy chow hall this side of the Pearl Harbor Sub Base," Redneck said.

"UH, OH! We're in deep ca-ca now!" the pilot shouted over the intercom. "We've got incoming ground fire! See them tracers off to the right—that's 'starboard' to you 'Swabbies.'"

On the advise of the helo Crew Chief, everyone took off their flack jackets and sat on them.

"When you're taking fire from that direction, your ass is the target that needs protecting," he told them.

Lucky for the team, they all had their seatbelts buckled, because the pilot began banking from one direction to the other in an effort to dodge the fire. His fighter-pilot maneuvering technique quickly carried them out of range of the hostiles, and the rest of the trip to Tan Son Nhut went without further incident.

Ensign Duncan welcomed Brady and his team back with: "OK, you Pirates. Clean and stow your equipment, get cleaned up, and get your film and data sheets ready for shipment. The good news is, we now have a Personnel Man who understands the military paperwork system. He can assist with the typing.

"When you've finished, you've got two days of stand-down before your next road show. Stay out of trouble, and be sober, ready to rock-and-roll at 0700 muster, Monday."

Friday afternoon and night, and on into Saturday noon, was spent catching up on sleep. Saturday night, though, with the whole team back in town, each man found his own method of untangling the knots.

Only one incident marred the week-end stand-down time—some of men decided to hit the EM Club at the Majestic Hotel and there, the beer flowed freely.

About midnight, Mad Man, having downed an enormous quantity of Bah-Me-Bah, decided he could swim across the river in front of the hotel. He was doing pretty well, until he suddenly found himself in the beam of a spotlight.

The 'ham' in him surfaced and he started making like Elvis, but quickly found out he was playing to an audience of 'White Mice' (Saigon Police). The River Patrol men had never heard of Elvis so had no appreciation for his performance. He was apprehended and hauled into their boat.

Ensign Duncan was less than pleased to have the police deliver Mad Man to the CCG Villa at 3 o'clock in the morning. The 'bail' (palm grease) settled on was a half case of cigarettes.

So, for the remainder of Mad Man's tour in 'Nam, he would be smokeless.

"You're damn lucky you didn't get your ass blown out of the water by those trigger-happy cops," Senior Chief Brady scolded. "Now, go take a <u>good</u> shower and put those wet clothes in a bucket to soak. 'Mama-San' will have to scrub them for two days to get the Saigon River crud out of them. We may just shit-can them, it'd be easier than trying to decontaminate them."

Monday morning, Ensign Duncan laid out their new projects. About half of the men were still nursing bone-splitting headaches, but everyone was raring to go.

"You guys know that I run a 'tight ship', but, no matter how 'tight' you got Saturday night, it's time to tough-it-out and get to work," Duncan told them.

"Mad Man and Ding-a-Ling, you're going along on a 'shufly' operation over the Delta. That's a Marine helo transport of ARVN troops. There'll be four helos going in. You guys split up, one in helo #1 and the other in helo #3. We want air-to-air coverage, and lots of stuff on the set-down and the troops disembarking at the LZ (landing zone).

"Stay with the choppers and return with them for a second load. Here's your contact at the Marine Air Wing Det. Be there, ready to go, at 0830. You've got three-quarters of an hour, so hop to. Stay lucky, keep your butts down, and come back safe."

With their instructions in hand, the two rushed off to gather their gear and head for the helo pad,

"Senior Chief Brady, you and the rest of your crew, will be picked up here at 1500 hours and taken up the river to the MRF

(Mobile Riverine Force) base and boat landing," Ensign Duncan said. "You, and your men will board the two AMSs (River Mine Sweepers) tonight, for their sweeps up and down the Saigon River. They'll make two sweeps, at 0100 and 1200. You won't be able to get much footage on the early morning sweep but you should be able to get some nice sunrise stuff.

"That's it guys. Stay alert. Hopefully none of you will get into any hostile action, but, if you do, keep your cameras rolling, your heads down, and CYA. (cover your asses)."

When Senior Chief Brady, A.J., Redneck, and Caesar arrived at the boat landing, they found it was a sprawling complex that had once been a fishing village. But, instead of fishing boats tied up to the docks, there were olive-drab, or camouflaged Swift Boats, outboard—propelled Zodiac rafts and various other military water craft.

Nearby was a barge that was the berthing and staging headquarters for a detachment of SEALs. Over the gangway, leading to the barge, hung a sign saying:

"Yea, though I walk through the Valley of the Shadow of Death, I fear no evil, for I AM THE MEANEST BASTARD IN THIS VALLEY!!"

And everyone in 'Nam—especially the VC—knew that to be the God's honest truth. The VC called them "The ghosts with green faces", referring to the green cam-ouflage paint they wore. No VC relished meeting up with them.

At the extreme south end of the nest of boats was a larger pier where two wooden, gray minesweepers were moored. These were the ships that, twice a day, swept the river for underwater mines, which the VC delighted in replacing as soon as they had passed.

The river was the main supply line to Saigon, and ships, large and small, were constantly traversing it's waters. Several ships had been damaged by the VC mines, and those beyond saving were run aground out of the main channel. The larger ships limped on into Saigon for repair.

The team checked in and were briefed on what to expect.

"We usually have it pretty quiet on our runs. The jungle, along the river, has been defoliated back about a hundred yards inland, so they don't have much cover, if they do try to slow us up," Chief Bo'sn's Mate Roberts, skipper of the lead boat, announced.

"Each boat has a .50 caliber in the aft gun tub, and we have five .30 caliber machine guns we break out and mount on the rail stanchions. We also carry two M-79 grenade launchers and four to five M-16s. Our six-man crew, four on deck and two in the engine room, can throw down some pretty heavy fire power, if needed. You guys will be expected to man weapons also, in addition to your photography. Any questions?"

"Yeah, Chief., About how long does it take to make the run down to Vung Tau?" A.J. asked.

"Right around six hours, if we don't snag any mines and have to stop to dispose of them. We normally get back up here in time to start our second run at about 1200.

"If that's all, you get some chow, relax, and we have a pretty good movie this evening. Just hang loose. We board at midnight, and don't miss the boat."

"We should get all our gear aboard now, so there won't be a last minute rush, and we forget something," Brady informed his men.

"After we finish," Caesar said, "I'm going over to the Master-at-Arms shack.

Some of the guys have a ten-foot long Anaconda they caught by the garbage dump this morning. I want to get some pictures of that."

"Just don't get too close, Caesar," A.J. laughed. "He might wrap himself around your tubby little belly and pop you like a pimple."

"Hey, I'm known as the 'Clyde Beatty' of South Chicago. I used to catch all kinds of 'critters' and keep 'em for pets. I've handled everything from snakes to skunks, and never got bit or pissed on."

"There's a first time for everything, Little Buddy. And if they should have any skunks, you'd best not come back here stinkin' up the place. You're bad enough, after two or three days in the jungle, so we don't need anything added."

"I'm goin' with him. I ain't never seen one of them big worms, except in the Tarzan movies," Redneck said.

The two went off in search of the snake while A.J. and Brady proceeded to explore the rest of the camp.

At midnight, Brady and Redneck boarded the lead ship and A.J. and Caesar climbed aboard the second one, and they all settled in for a 'cruise on the River'.

Underway at 0100, the first run to Vung Tau, at the mouth of the river, was quiet and uneventful. The weather, which had been raining earlier in the evening, was clear, and, on the water, a cool breeze made the trip very pleasant. The para-vanes, designed to catch and cut loose any mines as they trailed behind the ships, brought up nothing on the first leg nor on the return to Saigon.

Brady spent the time doing stories of the ship's crew and photographing them at their duties, which consisted mainly of tending the para-vane towing cables, and keeping a sharp lookout for debris in the water that might snag them.

Redneck was catching the action with his 16mm Arriflex and the trip was going off without a hitch.

The two ships turned around and started the second sweep down-river at 11:45 A.M., fifteen minutes ahead of schedule.

The second run appeared to be going as smooth as the first, until they approached a sharp horse-shoe curve in the river. They were about a half a click (km) from the bend, when the rattle of small arms fire could be heard in the scrub brush.

Brady and Chief Roberts were on the exposed upper pilot-house deck, and Brady commented to the Chief: "Sounds like someone's got a little fire-fight going on down there, Chief."

Before the Chief could reply, Redneck, who was on the main deck just below, hollered, "Hey, Chief, THEY'RE SHOOTIN' AT US!!" and pointed to splashes in the water off to the starboard.

"EVERYBODY, MAN YOUR BATTLE STATIONS, and stand by!! "Brady, if you know how to handle that M-79 grenade launcher, grab it and be ready to lay it on them. I've got to radio Saigon for permission to return fire."

"Grey Fox, Grey Fox, this is Mike-Sugar-One, Come in. Grey Fox, Grey Fox, this is Mike-Sugar-One, come in."

"*This is Grey Fox. Go ahead Mike-Sugar-One.*"

"Grey Fox, we're taking fire from coordinates 2-6 Victor Tango. Are there any 'friendlies' in that zone?"

After a long pause, which seemed to go on forever, the radio crackled back:

"*Negative, Mike-Sugar-One, no friendlies in 2-6 Victor Tango.*"

"Grey Fox, request permission to return fire on hostiles."

"*Standby, Mike-Sugar-One.*"

"Chief. They're goin' to have us zeroed-in any minute," one of the deck hands shouted the alarm, as more rounds splashed within inches of the boat.

More anxious minutes dragged by, with the ship fast approaching the dangerous fire perimeter. Finally, the answer came back:

"*Permission granted, Mike-Sugar-One.*"

"FIRE!!" Chief Roberts shouted.

The .50 caliber roared into action, followed by three .30s on deck and the Chief's .30 caliber, which he had mounted on the rail post on the open bridge. Brady started lobbing M-79 grenades into the brush on shore.

The rain of bullets and grenades tore at the leafless brush, cutting everything to flying chips. Still no enemy gunners were visible. The intense firing continued until the first ship had rounded the curve in the river. In their wake, the second ship was also tearing up the landscape where the original hostile fire emanated.

The only casualty during the exchange, was A.J. As he was reloading his weapon, the gunner standing next to him, swung his .30 caliber machinegun around to place a new ammo belt in the breech. The hot barrel seared a line across A.J.'s bicep, leaving a pencil-thin blister where it made contact.

As the second ship rounded the bend, two 'Huey' UH-1 Gunships came out the sky spraying machinegun and rocket fire into the jungle.

"It sure took long enough for Saigon to let us defend ourselves, Chief," said Brady. "We could have been nothing but ripples on the water, if those 'dinks' had had any heavy armament, like a ChiCom 82mm mortar, or a RPG (rocket-propelled grenade).

They'd have blown us to bits, at the range we were, before they finally allowed us to shoot back!!"

"I read you, LOUD and CLEAR, Senior Chief. This is a 'war (?) of control'. All the 'Brass' at MACV HQ want to control every situation, big or little, and all the feather merchants back in DC want to control how we fight this 'war', too."

"There's so much 'control' from all directions, it's like dumping us in the deep end of the pool, tied up in a 'tote' bag," commented Brady.

Vung Tau was just an hour away and Senior Chief Brady decided his team should drop off there so they could get their pictures packed and shipped ASAP.

"How about sending a message to my guys on your other ship, to get set to disembark at Vung Tau? We have to get this stuff on it's way to Chinfo while it's still 'hot' news."

"Will do, Senior Chief."

There were no further incidents and the two ships soon pulled alongside the rickety pier. The photo team made a quick leap to shore, passing their cameras and gear, hand-to-hand. Two Navy Shore Observers from the tower on the hilltop, were waiting with a Jeep, to take them to the small Naval installation a mile inland from the point.

Two hours of typing data sheets and captions, wrapping, and labeling and the film was ready to go on the first plane out of Tan Son Nhut.

While waiting for Brady to arrange transportation, A.J., Redneck and Caesar spent time downing a beer (or two) in the EM Club, which, by day, was the mess tent. They struck up a conversation with the base Hospital Corpsman, and, during the exchange, Caesar mentioned A.J.'s accident.

"Hey, AJ, you need to come over to the sickbay tent with me and let me dress that. Any kind of open sore can easily get infected, in this climate. No sense in taking any chances."

A.J. reluctantly allowed the Corpsman to clean and dress his arm.

"This is no big deal. I feel foolish making something out of such a piddling little blister."

"Nothing's 'piddling' out here in this bug-infested country, A.J.. Now, here's the medical report. When you get back to your parent command, submit this for your Purple Heart."

"Purple Heart!!?? Man, this wasn't done by those little ambushing Commie bastards! I just got my big ass in the way of that chief of the boat's gun barrel!!"

"Well, the regs say, *'any wound or injury received while engaging the enemy'*. Sounds like it fits the circumstances, to me."

"Hell, I'd feel like a real woosie if I accepted a PH for this. Forget it!!"

"Let me tell you something that happened just last week. We had three crew members from a 'Swift Boat' in here. They were the lead boat backing up a sweep across a point of land in the Delta, when their boat took an RPG round in the pilot house. It killed the helmsman, instantly. He fell across the wheel and the boat ran aground.

"They moved him aside and jockeyed the throttles trying to back the boat into the stream, but it wouldn't budge. They radioed the second 'Swift Boat' to come to their rescue, but they were heavily engaged and couldn't break loose.

"These guys were forced to submerge themselves in the swamp until sundown, and then, making their way down river, where they were picked up by the other boat. The three that checked in here were covered with leeches, and I had to remove them and treat them with antibiotics. Their CO awarded each one of them <u>Purple Hearts</u>!! And you think your wound is insignificant? Ha!"

"I'd still feel like a woosie. And that's the end of that!"

Brady gathered the team around, and announced: "I've arranged a hop for us on a Canadian Canberra first thing in the morning, so get your gear rounded up before you hit the sack. Give me all your exposed film and your data sheets, so I can get it packed ready for shipment as soon as we hit Saigon. We load at 0700, SHARP, and, they won't wait!"

TEN

Arriving back at Tan Son Nhut, they learned that Mad Man and Ding-a-Ling hadn't fared much better on their mission with the 'shufly' helo flights into the Mekong Delta.

The first two runs went off without a hitch. On the second wave, however, the ground fire was buzzing around the helos like an angry swarm of bees. ARVN troops had just disembarked, and the helos were lifting off, when Mad Man's craft took a round, which knocked out the hydraulics and sent the helo into an erratic spin.

"GRAB HOLD! And get ready for a hard landing! I don't see anything but trees down there, so, start praying," the pilot shouted over the intercom.

The helo took a hard dip to the right and the rotors started chopping leaves and branches out of the treetops. The fuselage hit the trunk of a sloping palm and started to slide down it like a roller-coaster car on it's first long drop. The tree managed to lessen the final impact, somewhat, and the crew was able to crawl out of the wreckage with a few minor cuts and scrapes.

Mad Man, though, wasn't so lucky. Being positioned closest to the door, he was whipped by branches and, when the craft came to a stop, his gunner's safety-belt tore loose and he was catapulted out, breaking his wrist and scraping some hide off his forearm.

"I think the radio is intact," the pilot announced. "I'm going to call in a rescue bird and we should be out of here before dark—I HOPE!"

The gunner grabbed the first aid kit and covered Mad Man's lacerated arm and, with some seatbelt webbing, rigged a sling to support his wrist.

The crew-chief popped a smoke to mark their location to the other 'shufly' helo, then got off a call for assistance.

"Shufly-two, Shufly-two. Mayday, Mayday. This is Shufly-one. We're down. Send rescue. Marking location. Mayday, Mayday."

"Roger, Shufly-one, 'Angel' on the way."

The rescue helo arrived within minutes, but was unable to make an extraction due to the dense jungle cover.

"Shufly—One, Shufly—One, this is 'Angel—Zulu—One', we see your smoke but we can't get the 'penetrator' skyhook through all the trees. There's an opening about one hundred meters north of your position. Can you make it?"

"Angel—Zulu—One, we receive and will proceed to the clearing. Heavy undergrowth will make it slow going, so don't go too far away. We'll radio when we get there. Enemy forces are concentrated two sectors to the east, so stay clear of that area. Over and out."

Fighting their way through the tangled underbrush was hot and tiring work. Mad Man was on the verge of passing out from loss of blood, so required assistance keeping up. Their determination paid off and they were able to claw their way through and reach the small clearing after about an hour's struggle

The clearing proved to be too small for the rescue helo to land, so, they had to be hoisted aboard, one at a time. The pilot was the last man and as he was being hauled up, enemy troops arrived and began firing. The rescue pilot didn't wait for the sling to reach the hatch, but, instead, yelling for the 'Shufly' pilot to: "**HANG ON**", he lifted off and flew away with him still dangling at the end of the cable. He was a swinging target but still received two hits in his gluteus maximus (buttocks). He was thankful to finally be up and out of range. The helo crewman wasted no time in activating the hoist and dragging the pilot aboard.

"Man, I felt like one of those little ducks running back-and-forth in a carnival shooting gallery. I'm sure glad those 'gooks' never hunted ducks back in Minnesota."

His wounds turned out to be superficial, but it took him out of the pilot's seat for a few weeks, and got him some R&R (rest and recuperation) in Bangkok.

Mad Man's break was clean, but, his forearm needed further treatment. He was flown out to the Hospital ship off shore, where specialists could patch him up better.

Much to Mad Man's dismay, his were not 'million-dollar' wounds (serious enough to send him 'stateside') and the doctors told him he'd be back on duty in a week or less. Mad Man did get the distinction, though, of being the first Navy combat cameraman to be awarded the Purple Heart in Vietnam, if you discount A.J.'s refusal to accept one.

Ding-a-Ling arrived back in Saigon, not knowing if Mad Man had made it, or not.

"I saw his helo go down, but we 'dee-dee mau-ed' out of there so fast, I couldn't see who got out. We caught their 'Mayday' and passed it on to 'Angel-Zulu—One,'" he told Ensign. Duncan.

To everyone's relief, the report of the rescue was forwarded to the Saigon CCG Detachment HQ before the end of the day.

"Men, I just got the good news. Mad Man's going to be all right. He's got a broken wrist and the hide peeled off his arm, but, we'll have his ugly puss back in a few days," Ensign Duncan informed the troops, when he got off the phone. "He's aboard the Hospital ship where he's giving the doctors, and especially the nurses, the benefit of his vast knowledge of what tickles the 'funny bone.'"

"Too bad he didn't get to go back to 'The World,'" Little Caesar remarked. "Now we'll have to put up with his 'B.S.' and tall tales 'till the end of the tour."

"Senior Chief, do you suppose we could go out to the ship and visit him?"

Ding-a-Ling asked.

"It's funny you should mention it, Ding-a-Ling. I was just thinking the other day, 'we ought to do a story on the Hospital ship out there'. What do you think, Sir?"

"I think its a 'bitchin' idea, Brady, and I think there's enough going on, that we'll probably need all of team Alpha-One to do the job right," replied the Ensign. "Set us up for the first available flight of the shuttle helo. And book me, too. I think his O-in-C should be the one to present him his Purple Heart."

"Aye, Aye! Sir!"

"Lordy, he was hard enough to live with before. Now we'll have to listen to: 'How I Won The Purple Heart', until eternity," said Caesar.

Due to a heavy load of casualties, the team had to wait two days for space on a flight. Time which they spent cleaning their cameras and getting their laundry done.

When they were finally aboard the helicopter headed for the Hospital ship, they marveled at the serene beauty passing beneath them. The lush, multi-hued, greenery of the jungle and the blue ocean, with it's whipped-cream-topped waves breaking, and then gently kissing the broad, sandy beach. It was difficult to imagine that, under those trees, men, women, and children were killing and maiming each other.

"Senior Chief, when this ruckus is all over, no matter how it goes, some smart-assed capitalists are going to come over here and build hotels and condominiums on those beaches. They'll turn all this beauty into another Waikiki or Bahamas resort, and get filthy rich. Just watch and see.".

"Sure they will, Caesar," A.J. chuckled.

"Go ahead and laugh, but, I'll bet a month's beer and cigarette rations on it. I just wish I had the dough to do it <u>myself</u>!"

"If it's such a sure thing, why don't you get some of your Chicago 'wise guy' friends to stake you?" Ding-a-Ling asked.

"HA! Now <u>that's</u> funny," A.J. snorted.

By this time the helo was settling down on the helo pad on the stern of the ship, and the discussion ended.

As they climbed out of the plane, they were met by two officers. The senior one, a Commander, introduced himself.

"Welcome aboard, men. I'm the ship's Executive Officer, Commander Taggart, and this is our Public Affairs Officer, Lieutenant Polaski. We're glad to have you and your men visit us, Ensign. My crew and medical staff could use some publicity. They're doing a bang-up job saving lives and limbs and I'd like to see them get some credit for it. Whatever you need, 'Lieutenant. Ski' here will make sure you get it."

"Thank you, Sir." Ensign Duncan replied, as he snapped the Commander a sharp salute.

Lieutenant 'Ski' led the team down a passageway towards the middle of the ship.

"We'll get you and your men fixed up with bunks, and, then I'll take you to see your buddy. I know you're all anxious for him to get back 'in harness', and so are we. He has the whole ship, and especially the nurses, rolling in the aisles, with his wise cracking and goofy shenanigans. We'll be a month getting them settled down to the serious work at hand. Don't get me wrong, we need some lightheartedness, occasionally, and he's been 'just what the doctor ordered'. Everyone likes him, but they think he's a nut case."

"We sympathize with you, Lieutenant," Duncan replied. "He takes a lot of getting used to."

The photographers were assigned bunks in the crew's berthing compartment, Brady in the Chiefs' Quarters, and 'Lieutenant. Ski' put Ensign Duncan up in a spare bunk in his stateroom. After dropping off their camera equipment in the Public Affairs Office, they were escorted to the patients' lounge, where they found Mad Man regaling a group of patients and staff with his Henny Youngman routines. Everything came to a halt, though, when he spotted all his buddies trooping through the hatch.

"**HEY!** Would you look what the polecat just drug in! Come to pay homage to the

'hero of the Delta', did'ya?"

"See, I told you he'd be insufferable," Caesar said. "It's starting already. He's even worse than ever!"

"Hey, I gotta milk it for all I can, while I'm a 'casualty'. I get back on 'the beach' and I'm just another one of those 'Crazy Camera Guys'. Sure good to see you Shitheads, though."

"Is that any way to talk in front of all these pretty nurses?" A.J. admonished him.

"Sorry 'bout that, Ladies."

"To tell the truth, we're here to tell the saga of these marvelous, medical, miracle workers. Seeing you was just an accident of poor timing," Caesar said.

"Caesar, Get fu . . . , Oops, Sorry ladies, I almost slipped up again."

"Gather around, guys, Mr. Duncan has something to say to this goldbrick.," Brady announced. "Sir, the floor's all yours."

"Thank you, Senior Chief. Ahem! . . . Hurumph! . . . By diligently <u>not</u> following Navy Rules of The Road, to wit, hanging his butt out the hatch of a helicopter while said helicopter is crashing through the jungle tree tops, and in the finest tradition of the Combat Camera Group, Detachment Alpha-One (better known as 'Those Crazy Camera Guys'), the motto of which is: '*I don't give damn how you do it, just get the picture!*', and in so doing you broke bones not connected to your cranium, (too bad, it might have knocked some sense into that thick skull), you have earned the Purple Heart and a solid 'Bronx Cheer' from all of your jealous teammates. Being we are all of unsound minds but whole bodies, I take pride in being the one to pin this medal to your open-back hospital gown, for all to see and touch (the medal, not your flabby backside!)

CONGRATULATIONS!"

"We would all break out in a loud cheer, but the sign over there says: '*Quiet, Hospital Zone!*'" A.J. commented.

"No champagne and caviar? Not even cookies and milk, to commemorate this momentous occasion?" Mad Man complained. "Some party this is!"

"Keep that up, and I'll break something besides your wrist," warned Caesar.

"OK, Guys. Speaking of 'breaking' things, we need to 'break' this up and 'break' out our camera gear. Our 'break' is over. Time to get busy," Brady told the men. "First off, I think we'll blend-in better, if we all change into working summer whites and khakis. We stand out like sore thumbs in these jungle fatigues. Remember the first rule of documentary photography—'be inconspicuous.'"

"I concur, Senior Chief," said Ensign Duncan. "Lieutenant 'Ski' has listed all the important departments to cover. So get with him to pick your 'targets.'"

"I think I'll see what story possibilities might present themselves among the patients and staff in the post-op ward," Brady said.

A. J. opted for the helo-pad and air-med-evac crews. His brother had flown medical helicopters in Korea, and was credited with rescuing 73 downed airmen, which earned him three Air Medals, so he held a close camaraderie A.J., himself, had applied for flight training but was turned down because of his size. He just couldn't stuff his huge frame into the cockpit. His interest in flying since early childhood, gave him an insight into these 'flying medics'.

"Well, Caesar, I guess that leaves you Redneck and 'Ding-a-Ling' to cover the ER and trauma center," Ensign Duncan pointed out. "Just keep in mind, you should concentrate on the ship's crew and the medical staff. We don't want to show the patients' injuries, if it could cause the folks back home undue pain and worry.

"That goes for you other guys, too. Keep it up-beat and positive."

"Aye, aye, Sir," they all responded.

The team spent the rest of the afternoon, and the following morning digging for stories, photographing and interviewing dozens of men and women who were the medical 'Angels' aboard.

When the time came to catch their flight back to Saigon, the men made one last stop to visit their buddy, 'Mad Man'.

"Hey, gang. You wouldn't believe this, but, this morning the nurse came in and told me to follow her, she was going to weigh me. I told her, "Hey, wady, I'd wike that, but isn't that a widdle non-regulation?"

"Holy Crap! He's back to his old 'cornball' self, already," Little Caesar marveled.

"Tell you the truth. You guys were sure a sight for sore eyes, when you walked in here yesterday," he told them, "For a couple of minutes back there, when that helo was making like a runaway toboggan, sliding down that palm tree, I thought I was a goner. Now, the Doc says I'll be back on the job in a few days. So don't do anything that I wouldn't do. When I get back we'll all do it together."

"Hell, there ain't nothing I can think of that he wouldn't do—and then brag about it," Caesar came back at him.

"I'll pass on that one, Caesar, but I mean it. I'll see you mugs, soon."

"I don't doubt that, Mad Man," Brady replied. "They tell me they have one of the best plastic surgeons in the U.S. Navy aboard. He had a very lucrative practice in Beverly Hills and left it to volunteer for this duty. He says the skin grafts on your arm are taking real good, and you'll be off the binnacle-list very shortly."

"Despite 'Little Caesar's' feelings, that's great news," remarked A. J.. "See ya soon, buddy."

"Yeah, I guess the Ladies in white are going to have to do without me. I need to get back on the job and get you guys back in shape, while there's still enough left of the Team to salvage."

"What I hear from the nurses on board, your 'make-out lines' are pretty lame," Caesar laughed. "They can't tell the difference between them and your comedy routines."

"OK, Knock it off, you eightballs," Brady scolded." We have a helo to catch."

ELEVEN

"Welcome back, Sir. How's the 'Mad Dog' doing?" Teacher asked.

"He's going to be OK, Teach."

"Yeah, he's too crazy to be benched very long," Caesar added. "He'll be back regaling us with his heroic adventure, in a few days."

"By the way, Mr. Duncan, Lt. Oswald, 7th Fleet PAO, said to have you check with him as soon as you returned."

"OK, Thanks, Teach. I'll step next door and see what Oswald has for us."

"I want all your film, data sheets, and stories on my desk and ready to ship, before secure time," Senior Chief Brady announced. "A. J., you and Caesar stand by to run it over to Outgoing Freight, when it's ready. I want it on the first possible flight. That comes first, so hold off on the maintenance. You men can take care of your gear later, or first thing in the morning."

Most of the paperwork had been typed up before departing the ship, so the task of packing it up for shipment, was accomplished in short order.

"Come on, you pea-brains," Littler Caesar urged, "I want to finish with this crap, and get over to the NCO (non-commissioned officer's) Club and down a few 'cool ones'. I've had all I can take of those sodas and juices we got aboard ship. I want a few brews."

"I'm with you on that one, Caesar," A. J. answered. "I've been dry too long."

"I'm dry, too," Redneck said, "I couldn't whistle 'Dixie', right now, if General Lee, himself walked in."

"Now, don't everyone go gettin' yourselves 'snockered', tonight," Senior Chief Brady warned. "Mr. Duncan prides himself on running a tight ship, but he sure doesn't mean <u>that</u> kind of '<u>tight</u>'. We may have to be bugging out on assignment soon, so I want each and every one of you beer-hounds sober and ready to rock-and-roll, when we get the word."

"Don't worry, Senior Chief. Tonight we get our whistles wet, but, in the morning, we'll be ready to whistle any tune they play, 'Dixie' or 'Anchors Aweigh'," A. J. said. "Right now, I'm as dry as a popcorn fart. I couldn't pucker up, even for Marilyn Monroe!"

"Forget the skirts. I need a beer a whole lot worse than I need poon-tang.," Caesar declared.

"As much I could use both, I have to side with you, this time, Caesar. Come on, let's get this package over to the freight office, and hit the Club. We'll see the rest of you turd-heads there, ASAP."

Ensign Duncan returned just as they were heading out the door.

"Hey, hold on. Where are you two off to, in such an all-fired rush?"

"We're running our film and stuff over to Outgoing Freight, then, it's off to the NCO Club," A. J. answered.

"Fine, but, stop by here before you hit the Club. I have some important info to pass out to everyone, while you're still moderately sober. It'll only take a few minutes."

"Aye, Sir. Then, after that, why don't you join us for some refreshment?"

"Sounds good to me, A. J., but only a couple. See you back here in a 'skosh' (Japanese for 'a little bit')."

Caesar and A. J. hopped in the crew's van, with Caesar at the wheel. The tires threw up gravel, for twenty feet, and then bounded forward, responding to their rush to complete their delivery and get back to the Club.

"I sure hope that van survives you 'hot-rodders,'" the Ensign moaned, "I had to kiss a lot of asses to get it. I wouldn't want to have to go through that, again,".

"Don't worry, Sir," Teacher tried to assure him. "Caesar claims he took driving lessons from one of the Chicago Mob's best 'wheel-men.'"

"Buddy, if you believe his tall tales about his 'connections', I have some prime LA property I'd like to sell you. It's called the 'La Brea Tar Pits,'" piped up Ding-a-Ling.

"Just so's he doesn't get stopped by the MPs, or be tempted to play 'chicken' with a tank," the Ensign worried.

The men resumed their equipment cleaning, and had all the gear ready for their next project by the time A. J. and Caesar returned, safe and unscarred.

"OK. Gather around, everyone," Brady ordered. "Mr. D. has some 'poop' to put out."

"Thanks, Senior Chief, for those eloquent words. OK. Listen up. Commander, 7th Fleet has sent an urgent message, instructing us to remove our CCG patches, and anything else that can identify us as members of the military press. Leave only your name tags and collar rating devices. The VC have decided our news releases are not in <u>their</u> best interests and have put a $1000 bounty on all military journalists and photogs.

"You guys need to keep on your toes, even in Saigon and aboard the base. That's about three-to-four years wages, to these people, and you can't be sure <u>who</u> might be tempted."

"Yeah, we heard rumors about that bounty, while you guys were out to sea," Teach added, "but we thought it was just that—rumors."

"Well, believe it! MACV Intelligence picked up some of Charlie's propaganda flyers, the other day, announcing the reward," the Ensign warned. "So be on your guard!

"And one other important directive from MACV—, you'll only be allowed to carry your weapons on the way to and from work.—NOT on liberty, and NOT in the Clubs.

"There's been several cases of 'wild-west syndrome'—guys playing 'fast-draw', or trying to settle personal differences with flying lead. So far, thank God, and <u>lousy aim,</u> no one's been killed.

"That's it, men. Tomorrow we'll see what exciting assignments are in our future. Any questions?—OK. Let's all muster in the NCO Club. The first rounds on me!"

"Coor's all around, Minh," Senior Chief Brady instructed the Vietnamese waiter.

"So sorry, Chief San, no have Coors."

"OK, make it Bud."

"No Bud, Chief San."

"How 'bout Busch?"

"No any kind stateside beer, Chief San. All gone."

"What the Hell is going on here?" A. J. asked, "Hey, Sarge!" he turned to the club manager, "What's this shit about 'No American beer'?"

"You got that right, Sailor. The damn VC blew up two barges coming up the river from Vung Tao, and it was just our piss-poor luck, they were loaded with our incoming beer re-supply," the Club Manager answered. "You'll have to settle for Bah-Mi-Bah for a couple of days, just until they finish off-loading the cargo ship that's carrying the rest of the brewski supply."

"Man! That sucks!" Caesar complained, tearfully. "My kidneys get all screwed up, when I drink that green, Gook beer. Guess I'm going to have to switch to vodka and OJ. Damn if I'm going 'on the wagon' all because of those fuckin' jungle bunnies!"

"Easy does it, Caesar. You know how you get on vodka," A. J. warned him. "Don't forget what happened with that water buffalo, up in Danang, the last time you got soused on vodka."

"What happened, A. J.?" Redneck asked.

"Shit. He went to bragging about how good a rider he was, and tried to climb on a water buffalo. He accidentally kicked him in the flanks, jumping aboard, and that big black bastard bucked once, and throwed him twenty-feet into the rice paddy. To top that, he developed a thorough dislike for Little Caesar, and took out after him. He chased his ass across about two acres of rice-paddy dikes until our 'Italian Cowboy' took refuge on top of the ruins of a block-house. He kept him cornered up there for nearly an hour, and we couldn't get him to leave."

Caesar had a hard time making himself heard, above the uproarious laughter that engulfed his CCG tablemates. "He was one <u>mean</u> <u>SOB</u>! It don't pay to try to fork no water buffalos. Don't worry, Guys, I'll go easy on the vodka, tonight."

"Gentlemen, I have an idea. Let's have one 'cool one' here, and then head for the villa. I've got a couple cases on ice, there, and we won't have to worry about who's sober enough to drive home," Teacher suggested.

"How 'bout we have a <u>couple</u> cool ones here. <u>Then</u> retire to the villa," Ding-a-Ling suggested.

"OK, Guys," Brady said, "Let's make the most of the situation. Pretend you're already too drunk to taste the Bah-Mi-Bah."

"That won't work for me," Redneck put in. "My taste buds get <u>more</u> sensitive when I'm bombed, But I'll hold my nose, and chug-a-lug it. Maybe it'll fool 'em."

The sun was just setting, when the van, packed to the window-tops with the photographers and four or five 7th Fleet Detachment sailors, arrived at the villa. The sight that greeted their eyes both startled and surprised them.

The street was cordoned off at both ends, with MPs and Canh Sat (Saigon police) stopping all traffic,—vehicles as well as pedestrians.

"Holy Jehoshaphat, Batman! What's happenin' here?" Caesar exclaimed.

"Stay in the van, you bums, while I see if I can get someone to tell me what's going on," Mr. Duncan ordered, as he slammed his officer's hat on his head and marched up to the senior non-com MP.

"What have we here, Sarge?"

"Good evening, Sir! It seems some VC or 'cowboys' (Saigon juvenile gangs) have been decorating a couple of the houses on the block, with some anti-American graffiti. Also, a witness across the street, thinks he saw one of them toss a bundle over the gate, before they took off on a couple of Vespas."

"We have a villa just two houses down, on the right—C 1214. Is it our place they hit?"

"No, Sir. It's two houses up from there, but they did spray-paint: '*Yankee Go Home*', on your gate. We have an Army bomb-squad on the way to check out the package. Until then, keep your people back behind the barricade, please."

The Ensign returned to the van and informed his crew of the situation:

"It looks like somebody might be trying to collect on that bounty. At least they know American GIs are living on this street. We're going to have to double up on security and keep our eyes peeled, 'til they round up these characters,.

"Senior Chief, you can get busy drawing up the new watch list as soon as we can get inside. I want the watch standers armed and wearing flack-jackets. Got that?"

"Aye, Aye, Sir."

"Man, I sure hope we don't have to move. I was just getting to know the neighbors," Redneck lamented. "Those little gals across the street, where we buy our ice, were gettin' real friendly. Every time I go in for a chunk of ice, they laugh and giggle, Real friendly people, they are."

"Redneck, do you know <u>why</u> they laugh and giggle when you tell them you want ice?" Caesar asked, stifling his own laughter, "It's that 'Gawgia' accent of yours. Every time you said you wanted ice—'*nouc da*'—it came out like you were asking for URINE!"

"Why the Hell didn't you guys tell me that? You let me make a Missouri Ass of myself. Here I thought I had somethin' going with those gals!"

"We didn't want to spoil the fun for those 'real friendly' ladies. It was probably the only good laugh they had in weeks. They needed the cheering up," chuckled A. J.

"OK, Ensign, you can take your people through, now. The package turned out to be a poorly made-up satchel charge, which failed to detonate. Good thing it didn't, too. It probably would have taken out most of the block. The Army guys are going to haul it to the boonies and set it off. We've searched the grounds around all of the villas and it's safe—for now."

"Thanks, Sarge. Sure glad we weren't home when it was delivered," replied Ensign Duncan.

"Take my advice, Sir, and start lookin' for new 'digs'. Never can tell when they might come callin', again."

"I don't think that'll be necessary. We're going to be twice as alert from now on. We'll be ready for them the next time. I'm checking with MACV in the morning, to see what kind of trouble we can get in, if we blast the next intruder that comes to visit."

"Yes, Sir. Just make sure you do the job right, so we don't have to come over and finish it."

Senior Chief Brady pulled the van up to their gate and Mad Man jumped out, unlocked it, swinging it wide.

"I want that crap painted over as soon as the sun comes up," Mr. Duncan announced. "Get someone from the Navy Civilian Labor Pool over here with a bucket and brush. Get me Michelangelo, Picasso, or Bonzo the monkey.! I don't care, and what-ever color it get's painted, is fine—so long as it isn't NAVY PEA-GREEN!!"

"I think we should call the game for tonight, guys. A party doesn't seem very appropriate, in view of the situation," Brady commented. "We'll make up for it another time."

With the dawn, came the monsoon rains. The muffled, regular 'Whoomf!', of the VC mortar harassment, mixed with the thunder of the tropical storm, presented an almost constant rumble. Raindrops, pounding on the roof, competed with the occasional automatic rifle fire heard in the city's suburbs.

Lien, the maid came in, shaking the rain out of her hair and showed her frustration with the weather. Her laundry would'nt dry today.

"Brady, San, job too much. Need help. Tomorrow I bring sister, OK?"

"I guess you're probably right, Lien, This bunch takes a lot of cleaning up after. Is your sister on the OK list with ComNavV?"

"Yes, Brady, San. Sister numba one cleaning girl."

"What d you think, Teach? You're the HNIC where running the house is concerned."

"I think it can be worked out, providing we can get them both for $2.50 a day."

"Two-fifty, OK, Chief, San."

"That solves that. We're going to have to take a break from shooting pix, but, this'll give us an opportunity to catch up on doing some major maintenance on our cameras and weapons," Ensign Duncan announced. "A. J., you, Ding-a-Ling and Redneck start stripping down all the cameras. Use low-pressure, compressed air to blow out all the accumulated sand and dust. then wipe them down with a light coating of WD-40. Give all the batteries a full charge.

"Senior Chief, you and Caesar do the same with the weapons. We want to be ready to 'rock-and-roll' as soon as this weather breaks."

"Man, I sure hope this crap don't last too long," Redneck moaned. "I don't like the heat, but, I don't like this 'California Mist', even more."

"Waddya mean, 'California Mist', Mountain Boy?" Ding-a-Ling asked.

"It 'Mist California' and hit Saigon.'"

"Senior Chief, did someone give Redneck a 'humor transplant' from Mad Man?"

"Don't worry, Ding-a-Ling. Mad Man's due back, day after tomorrow. Hopefully, he's used up all his old jokes and has some new material," Brady responded, "Now let's load up. The van weighs anchor for Tan Son Nhut in thirty minutes.

"When this foggin' out loud, lets up, we need to pay another visit to the DaNang Hospital project, and up-date the status of the construction. There's, also, a couple of other story ideas up in 'I' Corps, that Mr. Duncan heard about at the 'O' Club."

"Yeah, Senior Chief. For instance, there's an old 35-year, 'Sea Dog', Master Chief with the Beach Master Group up in Chu Lai. He's sixty-three years old, and still going strong. The Navy thinks so much of his ability and guts, that they made special exceptions to allow him to continue on active duty, for so long. He's almost two hitches over the limit."

"Sounds like front-page stuff, to me, Sir. Teach, you'll need to get the paper-work prepared and set up the flight availability."

The foul weather grounded everything for three days, and, when it finally passed, the 'word' came down that the DaNang trip was off.

At morning muster, Ensign Duncan announced the change in plans.

"Here's the latest 'poop', fellas. We've got two SEAL Teams hunkered down in the Mekong, that need to be extracted, Seems they were dropped just this side of the Cambodian border, to cut off a company of NVA moving into 'Nam. They turned them back, and, now, we've got to send in a couple of PBRs (River Patrol Boats) to pick them up. I want a man on each boat, to cover the operation. Any volunteers?"

"I'm ready, Sir," said A. J.

"Me, too," added Caesar.

"This won't be a picnic in the park, guys. The VC are still lurking around, trying to pick off these SEALs, and you'll be sittin' ducks out on the water."

"Hey! What are we here for, Sir?" A. J. asked. "Since that bounty offer, we've all got targets painted on our backs, and we're 'fair game', just about anywhere we go in this 'dinky dao'(crazy) country. Not much difference—samo-samo."

"OK. Get your gear together. Travel light. Carry only what you can stuff in your pockets, but load up with plenty of film. I want saturation coverage, still and mopic.

"Senior Chief, this's gonna be a night mission so you'll drive these two down to Nha Be to meet up with the PBRs at 1700 hours."

TWELVE

The two PBR crews were standing by when the photographers arrived, just as dusk was setting in. The crew of each boat consisted of four enlisted under a First Class Boatswain's Mate. The boats were heavily armed with three .50 Caliber machine-guns, several M-70 grenade launchers, and six or seven M-16s.

The Lieutenant in charge of the PBR Squadron greeted A. J. and Caesar and handed each a flak vest and a helmet.

"Wear these until this mission is completed," he instructed them. "They're not much protection, but they're better than having your bare faces hanging out there as targets."

"I just hope we don't have to go over the side with these things on, Sir," A. J. said. "These vests would make very effective anchors, as heavy as they are."

"Yeah, I ain't that good a swimmer, bare-ass. I don't need the added weight dragging me down," Caesar added.

"Let's hope we get in and out without any of us having to prove our water survival skills," the crew chief of the number one PBR said.

"Good luck, Guys. Keep your asses and heads down, and bring back some Pulitzer Prize stuff," Senior Chief Brady said, as he turned the van back towards Saigon.

A. J. realized this operation was a real challenge to their photographic skills. He knew the dark of a moonless night didn't make for good picture-taking. The only chance for <u>any</u> photography was if the night should be illuminated by tracers or flares, and that meant a fire-fight and the inherent danger of someone getting shot. Fear was ever-present in all their minds, but, as the Senior Chief had once told them, "If you ain't scared out there, you ain't payin' attention!"

"Get aboard, Sailors. We're shoving off," the chief of Boat One shouted, "We want to get to the pick-up rendezvous before moonrise."

Both PBRs spun away from the dock with a roar and threw up 'rooster-tail' wakes as they sped off into the channel and headed east into the dark, dense jungle maze of the Delta.

Underway the photographers were informed their target was a village along the river near the town of Chau Doc. The SEAL teams had cut off the NVA company's advance out of Cambodia and had routed them back across the border. Now the SEALs were holding the village awaiting pick-up by the two PBRs.

"*Peter-Bravo-Two, Peter Bravo-Two, this is Peter Bravo-One, do you read me?*"

"*Peter Bravo-One, this is Peter Bravo-Two, you're coming in five-by-five. We have you on our radar.*"

"*Roger, Peter Bravo-Two, we'll take the lead. You follow about fifty meters off our port quarter. When we reach the pick-up point,*" *you move in and retrieve the first team, while we cover you. Then we'll move in for the other team. You'll take the lead on the return leg."*

"Roger, Peter Bravo-One."

"Tiger-One, Tiger-One, this is Peter Bravo-One, do you read me?"

"Peter Bravo-One, Tiger-One, read you loud and clear."

"Tiger-One, we have two canoes proceeding to rendezvous. School is out at zero—two-hundred."

"See you in the play-ground, Peter Bravo-One. I have one walking-wounded for the first canoe."

"Roger, Tiger-One. From this point on, all units keep radio silence. Only emergency transmissions. You know the drill."

The coxswains of the two boats throttled back to stealth-running-speed, and the engines grew quiet.

Three hours of tense silence later, the lead boat's coxswain cut the engines and let the forward momentum carry the rescuers nearer and nearer the village. Boat two slowly overtook the lead boat and moved slowly towards the shoreline.

It was deathly still in the dark jungle. Nothing was moving. Even the night birds and the swamp frogs were silent. All life in the jungle seemed to be waiting expectantly for something to happen.

"I hope they're OK," the boat chief whispered. *"Keep a sharp eye out for the signal."*

He had barely completed his sentence, when a small, quick blink of a red flashlight appeared next to the small dock.

"Everyone stand by you guns. This could be an ambush. I'm going to slip up to the dock. Be ready to bring the SEALs aboard."

As the boat slowly drifted up to the dock, several shadows materialized out of the blackness.

"*Yellow Ribbon*," came a hoarse whispered signal, to which the coxswain whispered in return: "*Red Returning*".

Immediately the shadows slipped from the dock to the boat.

"*Is everyone here?*" asked the chief of the boat.

"*Team One's all secure, Chief,*" the Seal team leader replied.

OK, then. Hunker down and hang on. Take that wounded man below deck an lash him in a bunk," the coxswain warned. "*We're goin' for a ride!*"

Boat One swung wide and headed back down-stream, as Boat Two began loading the rest of the SEALs.

"*Have we got everyone?*"

"*All but our rear-guard. He's right behind us—OK, he's on board, now. Let's Dee Dee Mau!*"

The coxswain put the boat in gear, and silently proceeded to join the other boat. They had barely made the turn, when, from down-stream, a burst of machine-gun fire broke the quiet of the night.

"*Peter Bravo-One, we're taking fire from the south bank! My engineman took one in the hip, but it doesn't look too bad, but we're pinned down. We slipped into a small cove and have taken cover behind a pile of driftwood. That machine-gun is chewing up these logs like a beaver, though, and at this rate, we'll be in the open in seconds! Suggest you hug the south bank and slip in on their flank. By the muzzle flashes, it appears there're only two men manning the gun.*"

"*Good. We'll lob some grenades and 50 caliber in there and make short work of them, Peter Bravo-Two. We'll be in position in ten seconds. Be ready to make a run for it when we cut loose on those monkeys.*"

"Stand by with those M-79s and the 50. We should be right under their noses any second now. Let 'em have it as soon as you have a target."

All Hell broke loose when the boat's gunners opened up. The SEALs added their fire-power and the jungle was coming apart with all the raining explosives.

A. J. was using both hands to manipulate his Nikon and 16mm Arriflex. He could see the machine-gunners on the bank, silhouetted by the glare of the exploding grenades and the tracers. Two final blasts were direct hits, and the gunners' bodies were flung into the air, like GI Joe dolls. Silence fell over the jungle as their bodies splashed down in the river.

The action lasted only about five minutes, and then, just like that, it was over. Everything was quiet and the jungle returned to it's former peaceful, quiet, moonless night.

PBR number Two came out of it's hiding place with a roar, making a 360° circle around PBR One and fell into position for the race back to Nha Be.

"*Boy! One, you sure dusted those babies good for us! They didn't know what hit them. Thanks.*"

"*That'll cost you a round of beers, when we get in, Peter Bravo-Two.*"

"*That was worth a <u>keg</u>, Man!*"

"*Let's go home, boys!*"

"*Peter Bravo-One, calling Big Boat.*"

"*This is Big Boat, go ahead Peter Bravo-One.*"

"*Big Boat, this is Peter Bravo One. We have the lost orphans aboard and are homeward bound. We have two who need patching up, so have the bandaids ready.*"

The remainder of the race was uneventful and the PBRs sidled up to their dock, just as the moon was peeking through the treetops.

A. J. and Caesar excitedly compared notes as they disembarked.

"I didn't think we were going to get any photos, as dark as it was," Caesar said, "but, boy when you guys opened up on those VC, I had plenty of light. I had to make real short runs, though. Every time I raised up, chunks flying off those logs were buzzing so close, I could feel the breeze."

"When we cut loose, the whole place was damn near like daylight," A. J. added, "I think we got some real 'action' shots. Mr. Duncan sure oughta' love this stuff."

Senior Chief Brady was due to pick up the men in the morning, so, the boat crews made room for A. J. and Caesar to bunk in with them. However, the excitement of the river run had them so keyed up, they were sleepless 'till almost sunup.

Riding back to Saigon, the two regaled Brady with their stories, each one trying to top the other. Their constant chatter left them breathless by the time they arrived at the villa. It was all Brady could do to get them to slow down long enough to write up their reports, and get their film and data sheets made up for shipment.

"Boy, if we hadn't blind-sided that VC machine gun nest, Caesar, you wouldn't be here, today," A. J. chuckled.

"Oh Yeah, and if a frog had wings, he wouldn't bump his ass."

"As you were, you lean, hard jungle fighters. Save it for the next time the VC ambush you. I just got word that the 7th Fleet Det. is sending its C-45 plane to Bangkok in the morning and they have two open seats, and, since the rest of the crew will be heading for DaNang, if you want them, their yours. The nice thing about it is, the plane won't be coming back for three days. It'll be so nice and peaceful around here, for Mr. Duncan and Teach, without you two around."

"Hot diggity dog, Senior Chief. You got yourself two hot-to-trot liberty hounds rarin' to go," Caesar exclaimed.

"OK. Just keep out of trouble and enjoy your R & R."

"And enjoy we will, Senior Chief," A. J. smiled. "I don't know about the 'Rest' part, but we're definitely ready for some 'Recreation'!, Eh, Caesar?"

"You betchum, Kimosabe"

"Right. Well, get your cameras and weapons cleaned up and stowed away, then sack out. We'll be underway for Tan Son Nhut bright and early in the morning."

THIRTEEN

THE SUN WAS still below the horizon, but the sky was aglow with the dawn of a new day, when the team arrived at their Tan Son Nhut office. A brief stop to pick up their camera gear, and, they all piled back into the van.

Next stop was to drop A. J. and Caesar off at the flight line, where the crew of the 7th Fleet C-45, were going through their pre-flight inspections.

"I see you guys are rarin' to go," the pilot greeted them. "Throw your bags aboard and climb in. We'll be takin' off, shortly."

"Don't do anything we wouldn't do, you lucky dogs! Keep your hand on your wallet and your flies zipped!" Red Neck hollered, as the van sped away, to drop him, and the rest of the DaNang-bound crew, at the military air terminal.

DaNang had changed drastically since their earlier visit. Senior Chief Brady took note of all the new construction.

The rickety bridge they had crossed, risking life and limb, was now replaced by a steel structure, able to withstand the weight of two or three tanks.

A new base-camp, named 'Tien Sha', had been established near the road to 'Monkey Mountain'. All Navy administration and support activities were now concentrated within the secure camp.

The pot-hole-filled, rutted dirt road to the hospital, had been surfaced with marble chips, and, when they reached the hospital, it was no longer just piles of metal and lumber lying in the sand.

Several Butler Huts, containing an OR, a medical supply warehouse, three recovery wards with 40 beds each, a laboratory, staff barracks, a galley and mess hall, were completed. Work was still going on to increase the capacity, even more. Slabs had been poured for four more Butler Huts, (no more dirt or plank floors.) and eight permanent sentry towers, around the perimeter of the complex, were rising from the sand.

"We've got our work cut out for us, here, Guys." Brady advised his team. "To do this place justice, we need to work up a shooting schedule. There's a lot to cover and BuMed (Bureau of Medicine and Surgery) wants enough to make a comprehensive documentary out of what we shoot. We also have to plan for the dedication of the DaNang port facilities, the day after tomorrow."

After lunch, the hospital Public Affairs Officer met with the team.

"My name is Ensign Richard Mixon—that's with an 'M', if you please. I will be your 'go-between', while you're here. You men will have free run of the hospital, but, be sure you keep each department head apprised of your movements. Whatever you may need, to get your pictures, we'll try to provide. You'll have to 'gown-up' before entering the sterile areas, but that's about the only restriction on your movements." the young Ensign said.

"Thursday, at 1300 (1 PM), we're having our big Thanksgiving dinner, and you're all invited to join us. We have some damn good cooks here and, I hear it's going to be some spread. We also have a USO troupe scheduled for Sunday. You might want make time to fit that into your plans."

"Like I said, we've got a full boat, men," Senior Chief Brady added. "Mr. Mixon, if you have some time, We'd like to sit down with you tonight, and start planning this operation."

"I'm at you disposal, Senior Chief."

Three hours later, everyone was worn out and ready to turn in—but it was not to be. The night sounds were pierced by the screaming alarm.

Everyone grabbed helmets, flack jackets, and weapons and made a dash for the nearest bunker.

Red Neck dove for the first hole he came to. But that was a BIG mistake. What he took to be a safe refuge, proved to be a crater, left over from an 'invasion' the night before. The 'invaders' consisted of three or four pigs, wandering into the hospital area, being mistaken for crawling VC infiltrators. The sentries expended several grenades, eliminating the 'threat'.

Red Neck wound up, head first, in the resulting pit of mud and pig parts.

Tonight's 'attack' turned out to be a false alarm, also, and the 'all clear' siren brought everyone back to normal. Everyone, except Red Neck, that is. When he crawled out of his 'refuge', the men avoided him like a leper. No one wanted to go near him until he had showered three or four times, with strong laundry soap. Ding-a-Ling volunteered his entire supply of Aramis™, and Brady threw in his large, economy-size, can of spray deodorant. After a thorough dowsing with these, Red Neck was finally permitted back into the tent the CBs had provided for the team.

"Jeeze, Red Neck, I guess you learned not to stick your head into anything, until you've checked it out with your fingers, huh?" Ding-a-Ling chuckled.

"I'll tell you one thing, for damn sure, Ding-a-Ling. It'll be a long time before I have any appetite for bacon, hawg jowls, or chittlins.'"

"Georgia Boy, when I saw you crawl out of all the muck, I lost my appetite for FOOD OF ANY KIND!" Brady said. "I think I'd rather stand up and let the VC shoot me, than bury my face in decomposing pork. Yuck!!"

The next morning the troops were finishing off their morning coffee and assembling their gear, when—

"HOLY JUMPING HORNED TOADS," Ding-A-Ling exclaimed. "Where in Hell you been, Red Neck? You smell like some 'Cherry-Boy' from TuDo Street. What're you all slicked up for?"

"Well, I tried my damnedest to get rid of the stench of decayed pig and nothing seemed to do the trick. Then, last night, the CB cook told me about 'Mama's Pleasure Palace' just down the road. They got 'hotsie-tubs' and girls to scrub your back, a barber, and a 'while-you—wait' laundry service. I went for the works."

"You mean you dipped your wick, Gawgia Boy?"

"Hell, no! you sex-starved Chinaman! I ain't that hard-up—yet!"

Red Neck looked ready for inspection. His fatigues were starched and pressed with razor-sharp military creases, he had a close-cropped haircut and even his combat boots had a shine on them so bright you could see your reflection in them. But the greatest improvement was the sweet smell of lavender-water had erased his former aroma.

"For my money, you were long overdue for a good hosin' down," Ding-A-Ling remarked. "You know, Senior Chief, he doesn't change his socks until he can find them by the smell. He puts them under his bed to drive off the roaches and rats."

"You don't always smell so sweet, yourself, when you eat those over rotten eggs."

"Hey, in my culture, those are a delicacy. But then, your taste buds have been so petrified by so much 'hawg jowls' and possum fat, you wouldn't recognize gourmet food.

"I have an acute sense of smell, which has its advantages as well as its disadvantages. I can pick up on the odor of these nhuk mam (Vietnamese fermented fish sauce) eating VC at 100 yards. The downside is, I'm also supersensitive to bromhidrosis."

"What the Hell is bromy dose 'a piss, or whatever you just said?" Red Neck asked, in wide-eyed wonder.

"'Bromhidrosis', my backward friend, means **STINKY FEET**!!"

"Damn college-boys and their fancy-nancy words,"

Filming at the hospital, that day went very smooth, and Red Neck and Ding-A-Ling put aside their differences and fell to their assignments without another thought of the mornings' conversation. With Ding-A-Ling as first camera operator, Red Neck shooting 'fill-ins', and Brady picking up sound, with the Nagra recorder, they managed to cover most of the required scenes before sundown.

The following day, they interrupted the hospital project to cover the DaNang Port dedication ceremonies. It was pretty routine—speeches by South Vietnam VIPs, I Corps military brass, and U. S. contractors who built the piers and warehouses. This was followed by the usual ribbon cutting.

In addition to the festivities, the photographers shot several hundred feet of 'stock footage', of the port, showing its increased capabilities.

It now provided dockage for several cargo ships, and heavy-duty cranes for off-loading the equipment and supplies, directly from ship to warehouse. No more anchoring out in the harbor, and having to shuttle the cargo to shore, in landing craft.

On returning from the piers, Brady decided to move their base of operations to Camp Tien Sha, where there was more security.

Because they were mobile and subject to moving out on short notice, the Billeting Officer declined to assign them bunks, saying:

"I can't be tying up beds for your people, when I don't know when you'll be picking up and bugging out. I'll just sign your travel-orders 'No messing or berthing available', and you can scrounge around for sleeping arrangements. You can claim per-diem while you're here and buy your meals at the General Mess or the EM Club. Sorry 'bout that'"

"Aye, aye, Sir", Brady replied, "We're accustomed to being treated like unwanted step-children. Come on, Guys, Let's go find a place to perch."

They wound up 'perching' in the base photo lab at the invitation of the lab Chief.

"I can't offer you much, but we have plenty of floor space and some spare straw mattresses.

"We Photo Mates have to look out for our own," Chief Kelso told them. "I tried to get into CCG out of 'B' School (Advanced photo), but BuPers (Bureau of Personnel) told me I was more valuable running this lab. I envy you guys,—getting to travel all over the countryside, I seldom get as far as the DaNang airstrip to pick up supplies."

"Yeah, but you at least get three squares a day and don't have to eat them damn 'C' rations," Red Neck added.

"Speaking of which, are we going to partake of that promised Thanksgiving spread at the Hospital, tomorrow, Senior Chief?" Ding-A-Ling inquired.

"For sure, for sure, my little friend. We still have a few more hours of camera work to do over there."

As predicted by Ensign Mixon, the Thanksgiving Dinner was 'some spread.' The ships that had docked yesterday, had brought a hold full of turkeys, and all the fixins', to whip up a class 'A' meal for all the troops in I Corps.

The day gave the photographers a chance to do 'home-towner' interviews and some short 'family greeting' clips for local stateside TV spots.

'The only thing that could make this day better,' Brady thought to himself, *"would be, if all these men and women could be home, sitting down to this meal, with their families.'*

"New Plan-of-the-Day, Troops," Senior Chief Brady greeted the men at breakfast.

"We're flying out to the Carrier, USS Ticonderoga, at 1000 hours for a hush-hush operation. We'll get briefed when we get aboard. So, get all your stuff gathered up and fall-in at the Admin Office at 0930, ready to roll."

"You mean we ain't gonna stay for the USO show, Sunday, Senior Chief?" Ding-A-Ling asked. "I hear they got some NFL cheer leaders with 'em. Sure hate to miss that."

"Sorry-bout-that, Sailors, but we're going to be putting on our own 'show' in a couple days. Lottsa fireworks and maybe some swimming exercises."

"Hot Dawgies!" Red Neck wooped. "Now we'll get back to what we really came here for—some Pulitzer-winning action pics."

"Just keep cool, guys. This is Top Secret, so zip your lips." Brady admonished them.

He, too, was anxious for action, but, the thought of taking his team 'into harm's way' always gave him pause. He knew these men were ready and capable of doing an outstanding job, but, he feared for their safety. Brady couldn't help worrying about 'Murphy's Law'—'If anything can go wrong, IT WILL.'

He was always admonishing the men to "keep your head and ass down, but get the picture." In his heart and mind, though, no picture was worth any of his people getting hurt.

FOURTEEN

On the carrier, they were greeted by a Marine Lt. Col. And ushered off to the 'Ops' room for their briefing.

There, to their great surprise and joy, were Teach, A.J., Ceasar, and Mad Man, standing around the coffee pot, with Mad man regaling the ship-board sailors with his tall tales of the adventures of a combat-cameraman.

"Did you guys get tired of screwing off, and decide to rejoin us working stiffs?" Red Neck asked. "And what the hell are you doing here, Mad Man? I thought we had you off our backs for at least another three or four weeks."

"Sh-e-e-it, Mountain Boy. I wasn't about to miss this shindig and have you bragging all over the Pacific how you won this war, without me. The Doc said I'm a fast healer and turned me loose on you, goofballs."

"OK. Gather 'round, and listen up, Sailors. I'm Lt. Colonel Coltrane, gentlemen. I'm the Intel Officer for this operation. Here's the plan:

"Senior Chief, I want you to assign photo-mates to each of the landing parties. You'll coordinate with the company commanders of each group and follow their lead. Draw full battle gear from the Marine Quartermaster and make sure each man wears his when we go over the side. We won't be air-lifted in on this op. We'll go out through the cargo-hatch and down cargo nets."

"*Woops! My vast experience on the monkey bars, in kindergarten, is finally going to pay off,*" Mad Man whispered to A.J.

"*Pipe down, and pay attention, Asshole!*" A.J. scolded.

"Gentlemen, if I may continue? We've located a pocket of VC and NVA that've been harassing our troop and supply movements on the coastal highway. Our object is to land from the beach, while ARVN and our Special Forces hit them from the west. Give 'em the old 'Pincer' treatment. We going to squeeze them like a ripe pimple. It won't be a picnic, gentlemen. They're pretty heavily armed with mortars, RPGs, and even a few ChiCom recoilless 75s."

"Jeeze, Colonel, it sounds like a real hornets' nest," Brady observed.

"You got that about right, Senior Chief. Our best weapon is surprise—hence the reason for pre-dawn assault from both east and west. We'll get some cover from the two destroyers' shelling them from off shore as we hit the beach. It'll be coming just over our heads, so don't move forward too fast and over-run their target zone. The shelling will cease at 0600. That's when we advance.

"Any questions?"

"Yeah. Guys, if you don't understand the play, you'd best speak up now. In the morning it'll be too late," Brady said.

"My only question, Chief, is, where do we draw our armor-plated scivies?" Red Neck asked.

"Armor plate, or not, you best keep all your valuables tucked tight between your legs, and your cameras rolling!"

"One of the Marines in Ward 'B' has an AK-47 that he captured on his last patrol in the 'boonies,'" Ding-A-Ling told the Senior Chief, "and I have him talked into swapping it for my K-Bar knife and a half-dozen rolls of Kodachrome™. I think I'd rather be totin' that in a fire-fight, than my Colt-45. It's lighter, and, if, God forbid, I have to do any shooting, other than with my Arriflex 16mm, it'll sure lay down a heavier field of fire than the 45."

"Wouldn't mind having one of those hangin' on my shoulder, either," Brady agreed, "But let's hope we have enough support cover that we won't need to do <u>any</u> shooting. We need to concentrate on our <u>real</u> job and make sure we come back with the story."

"Hey, Ding-a-Ling. You best be mighty careful with that toy." advised 'Mad Man'. "A corpsman over in Danang told me about a 'grunt' coming in the Aid Station with a mangled hand. Seems he had a 'gook' weapon that he tried to test fire and it exploded and blew off his finger!"

"Jeeze," Ding-a-Ling yelped, "His whole finger?"

"No," Mad Man explained, "The one NEXT TO IT!!!"

"Where do you get all this crap, Mad man?," Brady asked.

"Hell, Senior Chief, that one brought down the house when Frank and Sammy pulled it off at the Sahara, a couple of years ago."

"Well, I can't say it's improved any, with age."

"That's all I have for you, tonight, Senior Chief. Reveille is at 0330, so you men get your stuff together tonight, and be ready to motivate with the dawn. Get some sleep. We're over the side at 0500. Happy hunting."

"Okay, you bums, before you hit the sack, I want to give you some pointers for tomorrow. Stick with your assigned parties. Get plenty of 'B' roll stuff and Taksan (lots of) close-ups. And try to get names and hometowns, where possible. The media eats that stuff up."

0200 (2am) Senior Chief Brady is awakened by the Flag Messenger.

"Senior Chief. Sorry to disturb your sleep, but Flag wants all the group leaders to meet with him in the forward mess decks, pronto."

"OK, Thanks Seaman, I'll be right there."

"Change in plans, Gentlemen. The 'weather guessers' have picked-up a doooozie of a storm coming down from the China Sea and heading our way. Therefore, the landing is scrubbed. We can't risk putting our boats in the water. The surf is going to be 10 to 12 feet and it'll swamp the small craft.

"We're proceeding back to Danang. ETA is about 1030. Gather your gear and prepare to disembark at 1100. Thanks everyone for your effort. Maybe we can do this dance again, sometime. Smooth sailing and following sears, Shipmates."

1300 THAT AFTERNOON—

"You men stay here on the dock with the gear, while I find a phone and call Ensign Duncan for instructions. Be back in a jiffy." and the Senior Chief took off towards 'The White Elephant' (nick-name for the white Navy Admin. Building in Danang.)

"I sure hope we head back to Saigon," commented Ding-a-Ling. "I could really go for a nice plate of snails at the le Admiral restaurant."

"Yuck," 'Little Ceasar' voiced his distaste. "How can you eat those slimy creatures?

"'Ceasar', they're not like the snails we've seen slithering around in the jungle. When they're sautéed up in butter and garlic, they taste a lot like Shrimp-Scampi. They're actually more tender than shrimp—more like oysters. You'd love them, if you ever got past the mental block."

"Hey, you numbskulls, here comes the Senior Chief. Now, maybe we can get to motoring out of here." 'Red Neck' yelled from up the dock.

"Guys, I've got some good news and some BAD news." was Brady's greeting.

"Oh shit, here it comes," 'Mad Man' growled under his breath. "I'll bet we're heading back out to sea."

"No such luck, 'Mad Man'. The **'good news'** is—Our relief crew is in Yokosuka right now, and they will probably be in Saigon by the time we are. Gather up our gear, The **'BAD NEWS'** is—**WE ARE ON AN AIR FORCE FLIGHT TO SAIGON AT 1630.** Next stop, the **U S of A!!**

Pandemonium broke loose among the photographers causing the others on the dock to just shrug and remarks were made about "Those CRAZY Camera Guys" were at it, again.

"The other good news is—our relief team will be waiting in Saigon, ready to take over the helm," added Senior Chief Brady.

"Whose team is it, Senior Chief?" A.J. inquired.

"Chief Gilmore's."

"Gilmore? Is that 'Gung Ho' Gilmore? I thought he retired two or three years back."

"He did, but when 'Nam blazed up, he volunteered to be recalled," Brady answered. "His feelings for the Chinese Commies go back to Korea and he jumped at the chance to 'get in a few more licks' at them."

"That's no great surprise. Senior Chief", 'Redneck' cut in.

"He has a real hard-on for the ChiComs," continued Brady. "He used to spend hours cussin' 'em out. He lost a couple of real close buddies who were with him in a POW camp. Almost died himself, from dysentery and a couple of other diseases. He doesn't talk much about his POW time, but I've heard he went through some real bad shit.

"He, and another prisoner were being transferred to another camp, when they managed to over-power their two guards, stabbed them with bamboo stakes and took off through the rice paddies and jungle.

"They were on the run for three days when they hooked up with a Marine company pulling back from the Chosen Reservoir. The whole bunch damn near froze to death before they were evacuated at Hungnam".

"I'll tell you," A. J. said. "I don't envy those guys on his team. He's out for blood so they'd best stay sharp. He's not reckless, but you can bet your ass, he'll be in the thick of the action every time out."

The two-hour flight south seemed like a millennium to Brady and his crew. When the C-130 finally landed, Senior Chief Brady lost no time in commandeering a Navy truck-driver and convincing him that it was a matter of National Defense that they get back to their villa. Of course, a promise of a case of American beer helped to clinch the deal.

There were three days of chaotic preparations, getting orders endorsed, settling up their Villa bills, buying the souvenirs they had neglected to get before departing, and. Oh, yes, rounding up their personal junk.

Red Neck almost queered their flight, when he insisted on dragging along his souvenir 'Boofy'. A 3ft., 70-80 lb., garishly-painted, ceramic elephant. ('Boofy' was the name GIs had tacked on the outrageous monstrosity—short for 'Big Ugly F—ing Elephant')

Boarding the aircraft, three days later, gave them all time to reflect.

With Brady, it was a feeling of satisfaction, knowing his team had completed all their assignments and he was bringing them back to their families, **alive** and **unharmed**.

His final thought, before settling back in his seat was:

"BRAVO ZULU" (Well Done)